KUNDU

The Prince of Riverton City

Courtney Ffrench

Three-Legged Elephant Publishing

DEDICATION

This book is dedicated to my children, Shiloh, Victor, and Anakin.

Daddy loves you.

Chapter 1

Shotta's Ball

Circa 1980
Riverton City, Jamaica

"It must be a rolling calf," Leon whispered, "only rolling calf can make those holes in his chest."

Lorraine looks over Leon's shoulder. She could see the men standing in a circle around a fire pit. The flames cast a shadow over the eyes of the men, leaving their pupils to sparkle.

"You ever see a rolling calf?" Kundu asked, from behind Lorraine.

"No, but my granny did see one, long time ago. She said it was big and black, he had blood and fire in his eyes and when he runs at you, you can hear the chain around his neck clanking louder and louder. Them can't die because them dead already."

Lorraine looks at Kundu as he gets down on his belly to look through the ripped zinc fence.

"Kundu," Lorraine squeaks.

He looks up sharply. "Shh!" He covers his lips with his finger. He motions to Lorraine to join him at the bottom of the fence, and Lorraine slinks down to the muddy ground. Kundu shifts over slightly, and she peers through the hole. Leon looks down at them, but then refocuses through the fence's top hole as the men started to fire their guns into the air.

There is a solitary white casket hung desperately over the bed of the rusting grey GMC pickup. The men are aimlessly walking around each other now as they casually reload their AK47s, Uzis, Glocks, and 357s. There are 20 or 30 men all dressed in white, some holding their ear with one hand and firing a gun with the other.

"Jeezam peez," Leon half shouts, as he goes to the ground next to Lorraine and Kundu.

"You really think it's a rolling calf?" winces Lorraine, covering her ears.

"Of course." Leon pulls up his pants that are three sizes bigger than him. His eyebrows furrowed with incredulity. "Marlon is the wickedest shotta. Them say him shoot about 40 people. A wicked boy that. A regular man can't kill him."

Kundu looks over at Leon, then at Lorraine, then back at Leon. "What about Sylvia, Doreen, Shorty, Peta Gaye, Trudy and Donna? You think rolling calf have them, too?" He pauses. "They just gone? Ghost bull stab them up? Nobody can find their body. A next shotta shoot him. Shotta kill shotta." Kundu looks through the hole again.

As the shooting stops, Lorraine stands up. "Somebody say Peta-Gaye probably ran away."

"Her father used to beat her hard," Leon interjected.

"That not true, though. She would tell me." Lorraine brushes gravel and brown sand from her hands and knees.

"Ghost, you have to go inside too?" asks Leon.

"Don't call him that, he doesn't like it when people call him that." Lorraine glares at Leon. Kundu gets up and brushes off his armpit-stained beige tank top. His shorts are cut at the knees from a brown dress pants. He has bowlegs. His eyebrows, eyelashes and hair are white. The pieces of rocks mixed with bottle caps had left various impressions on his white skin.

"Leon a big idiot, don't listen to him. I have to go home." Lorraine brushes half-dried mud off her hands.

"Kundu, you know some days your eyes are purple and another time they're red?" Leon smiles while looking over the fence at the now vacant lot. He turns to look at Kundu, who looks away.

Lorraine is standing between them. She is taller than Leon but slightly shorter than Kundu. She's dressed in a blue blouse with a grey skirt. The blouse has 'RN' printed on the left pocket and 'St. Francis Children's Hospital' printed on the right. She has brown skin with dark elbows and knees. Lorraine combs her coolie hair into two braids every day. It was the only style she had learned from her mother.

Light drifting smoke and the smell of burning steel lingered around them. Leon steps away from the fence. His skin is blue-black. He has on a large yellow Puma track suit that he wore almost every day. Leon has three patches of missing hair on the back of his head; the school nurse said it was ringworm. His lips are cracked and rough at the corners.

***

"No moon tonight." Kundu says softly. He picks up rocks the size of oranges and stuffs them in his pockets. "We're going to follow you to your yard."

He hands Lorraine two rocks. Leon picks up pieces of a broken cinder block. They walk from behind the fence onto the dirt lane in the darkness, and pass the smoldering fire pit. Kundu is in front, with Lorraine to his right and Leon to his left.

"What's that?" whispered Leon. He motions his chin towards the shadow diagonally across from where they were standing.

"I don't know," said Kundu. "Hurry up." He jumps over a hole in the ground and walks rapidly.

There is a woman in a white cotton dress and white head wrap standing with her back turned facing a narrow lane. She's standing barefoot in ankle-high mud and old newspaper.

"What she doing?" Leon stops walking, and Kundu and Lorraine halt behind him.

"She praying." Lorraine pulls Leon back towards her and Kundu.

"We can't go this way anymore?" asks Leon.

Lorraine shakes her head. "That's where Shorty and Donna were walking when they went missing."

Kundu nudges Leon with his elbow. "Ready?"

Leon re-grips his piece of cinder block. They all start walking sideways like crabs.

"Get ready to run if the gate is open," Kundu looks back at Lorraine.

"The gate is open," says Lorraine.

"Shh!" Leon cocks his hand above his head and shoulders, followed by Kundu.

As they pass the yard with the open gate, their walk turns into a trot, and then a full sprint. They giggle with relief as they reach the top of the uneven hill. As they get to the top, the woman in white walks away and disappears into the lane.

"Going to church tomorrow?" Lorraine breathes heavily behind Kundu.

"Not me," Leon mutters as he pulls up his wayward pants.

"I coming, but I have to stay outside," mumbled Kundu, as he looks down at his bare feet covered in soot and grey mud.

Lorraine squeezes between two barrels half full of rainwater, and walks toward the zinc, cinder block and plywood little house. There was a single light coming from the crack in the door. Kundu watches intently as Lorraine closes the door.

Leon has started walking down the lane in the dark. Kundu runs to catch up. They are walking stride for stride as they approach the yard with the open gate again.

"Let's start running now," Kundu says, and he takes off.

"Why?" Leon tightens the string holding his pants up above his waist.

"Head start. He probably won't know we're there until we pass the gate. Run!"

The boys are running downhill with both arms pumping. The thudding sound of bare feet on mud and gravel got louder as they passed the yard with the open gate. In seconds, a shadow flashed through the gate. Kundu and Leon are running with the shadow coming closer. Leon is looking behind intermittently.

"It's him!" shouts Leon. "It's Jomo." The dog gets close to Leon and snaps at his Achilles heel.

"Whayee," squeals Leon.

Kundu slides on loose gravel and then stops and turns around. He throws two rocks at Jomo. He fumbles for the others in his pocket. Jomo stops, walks in a circle, then stands still. Leon runs past Kundu, then stops to look for Jomo. Kundu hurls two more rocks that pass over Jomo's head. Leon angrily flings his broken pieces of cinder block.

Jomo stood still and stared at both boys, whose hands were on their knees, gasping for breath.

The dog looks away, then turns around and trots back to his yard.

"Guway!" Leon back slaps the air. Kundu throws away his last rock as they both walk away with tired legs and weak knees.

Chapter 2

Riverton City

Riverton City is a sprawling landfill, constructed into mountains of raw garbage. Garbage from the more affluent municipalities is piled here. There are mountains, some 30 feet high, made of plastic bottles, tires, newspaper, curtain rods, bed frames, odd furniture parts, dead dogs, refrigerators, rotten fish, toilets, Christmas trees, uniforms, car doors, cinder blocks, zinc fencing, and guns.

Post-colonial Jamaica has never had a particularly large middle class. If you were rich, you lived in the 'Beverly Hills' or 'Cherry Gardens' neighborhoods. If you were lucky and properly educated – which means attaining letters to your name - you could afford to live in an area with running water and fairly consistent electricity. For the majority of Jamaica, however, everything was uncertain: food, education, water, electricity, and safety.

Families that once lived off the land were forced off their farms to make way for an era of hyper tourism. Those that were ill-fated or could not meet the moment, found themselves in conflict with a society eager to look the other way. In so-called developed countries, its citizens believe they have a right to basic human dignity. In developing countries, for the poor majority, dignity is relative.

People looking for anything to trade, sell, wear, and cover themselves found an endless supply of possibilities in and around the Riverton dump. Roads were carved out by monster dump trucks that needed to access and traverse from one end of Riverton City to another. Eventually, homeless families would devise shelter and familial dreams for themselves out of cardboard, old mattresses, and cinder blocks. Soon and within one generation, families no longer recognize the stench: a decaying dog was no more grotesque than a rotten egg at breakfast.

Chapter 3

Madda Tee

Everything and almost everyone was asleep in the yard. The heavy rain punished the zinc roofs, and the winds joined in the foray.

Next door Ms. V lost her roof, and she kept screaming "Jesus Christ," over and over. The wind is even stronger tonight, and it forced itself through the creases of the unpainted cinder block walls. Kundu watched intently as the roof quivered and convulsed. Madda Tee's faded green kerosene lamp was standing insecurely at attention. It swayed and threatened the wet black floor.

The floor of the square house was an incidental litany of ideas that were never realized; part cement, part gravel, some dirt and tar, most of which was no different from the road that led to the compound. There was one lonesome window covered with warped rusted zinc. It had a thousand miniature holes that whistled and squealed all night long. The square room smelled of mackerel, kerosene, and wet cement.

The scent of salted mackerel with coconut milk was fading now. Madda Tee had made her famous Sunday Rundown: salted mackerel, coconut milk, tomato, caked salt, scotch bonnet pepper and sweet pumpkin. All the grandmothers in the yard knew how to make Rundown. Madda Tee showed Kundu once or twice, which always ended with her kissing her teeth. She would always say, "You afi get di tomato and mash it up. Yah lissen to mi?"

Kundu is laying on a flattened cardboard box that once held a refrigerator. Beneath the cardboard is a single, springless mattress, raised five inches off the floor by a dozen cinder blocks. His left arm hangs off, as his palm collects the droplets from a hole in the roof. The droplets tickle as they explode on impact in his palm.

Madda Tee lays motionless on her back, as she always does. Her bed was two box springs set on top of each other, and when she moved the springs would howl and crack. She had fallen asleep perhaps an hour ago after her tin cup of the night's cocoa. She had gathered her things and went to the low shed behind the square room for her nightly ritual.

The low shed was made of five varying shades of used brown wood, and the corners were affixed by silver nails. It had no roof. There was a wooden bench with a hole, ample enough to manage the bottoms of several extra-large grandmothers that lived in the adjacent yards. Next to the bench was a skinny pipe and silver faucet over a wooded drain that led into the weeds that grew independently behind the shed. She had emerged from the shed wearing her grey nightie with vines of faded purple lilacs printed diagonally across the front and back. The nightie was once white. She had also smothered her neck and chest with white powder; she loved white powder. Madda Tee loved white anything.

The nightie was a gift from her sister who lives in New Jersey. She had sent Madda Tee a barrel four years ago; it was filled with clothes, toothpaste, soap, lotion, deodorant, shoes, and candy. It was the first and last barrel she ever sent.

Madda Tee's sister was called Ms. Gurty. Everyone was called something other than their real name. She had slipped onto a boat heading for Florida. Somehow, she ended up in New Jersey and has lived there ever since.

The barrel eventually became the third piece of furniture. Inside, it had clothes for church. On the top of the lid there was a King James Bible wrapped in plastic, white framed glasses with one missing lens, a small picture frame with a faded photo, and a rusted gold goblet that Madda Tee got as a gift from the man in the faded photo.

Madda Tee would talk about Gurty to anyone, from the early sun until the whistling crickets came out for their midnight song. "Gurty sending for me enuh," she would say whenever she was annoyed, or Kundu did not behave like a Christian.

Kundu kept his eyes fixed on the roof. "Dear Jesus," said Kundu quietly, "please deliver us from our sins and trespasses, please forgive us for what we have done. Our Father, who ought in heaven, hallowed be thy name, thy rod and thy staff, they comfort me. Thou preparest a table before me, in the presence of my enemies. Thou anoint my head with oil, my cup runs over, surely goodness and mercy shall follow me all the days of my life. And I will live in the house of the Lord forever. Thank you, Jesus."

Chapter 4

Peta-Gaye

Sunlight bore its way under the space of the wooden door. It's a space that often invites blue ground lizards, snails, brown cockroaches, ticks, and scorpions. During the summer storm season, everything looks for a place to cotch.

Madda Tee is no longer snoring, but her eyes are still closed. "Go to Standpipe and get a pound a sugar," says Madda Tee. "Get the white one; the brown sugar too dutty." Her eyes are still closed. "Go to Ms. V and tell her to give you the money she has for me." Madda Tee sits up slowly. "Thank you, Father God."

Kundu opens the door to a blazing sun, and he immediately bows his head and looks away. There is no summer school this year and the children in the yard are emerging. The ground trembles as a dump truck rolls by; the slabs of concrete walls hanging over its gate, left a trail of white dust to settle in its path. Following the trail is an armada of higglers hoping to score something relatively valuable to sell.

Kundu is knocking on Ms. V's door. "Yes," replies Ms. V from behind the door. "Who is it?"

"Kundu, ma'am."

"Hold on." She opens the door. "Your grandmother still sleeping? She sick?"

"I don't know. She asked me to get the money, ma'am."

Ms. V digs into her pocket, then leans over behind her door and looks into her handbag.

"Here." She hands Kundu a dollar bill. "Tell her I'll give her the rest later."

"Ok," says Kundu. Ms. V is what the men in the area called '*healthy*' or '*tick*'. She washes clothes for an Uptown lady, and on the weekends, she higgles in the plaza near the rich people.

"Where you going?" says a voice from behind him. Kundu turns around, squints, and raises his hand to cover his eyes.

Leon walks down the plank from his door to the dirt.

"Standpipe, have to get sugar," replies Kundu.

"Want to go to the gully later?"

"After market." Kundu turns and picks up two long branches from the soggy uneven ground. They were left stranded by the wind in front of Ms. V's little house. Kundu breaks the branches into small pieces and tosses them into an incidental pile of wind-driven things, resting by the fence. Ms. V is locking her door. She has two crocus bags, one in each hand. She's wearing a faded blue denim skirt and purple halter top. Her rubber slippers are light blue, and her heels are grazing the ground as she begins to walk towards the gate of the yard. A police car pulls up and stops.

Two policemen in blue uniform get out of the front, and then two more dressed in military green get out of the back. The short dark-skinned policeman raises his palm to Ms. V and she stops by the gate. The three other policemen start talking to people just walking by, showing them a flyer.

As Kundu and Leon got closer to the fence, they could see the photo being distributed. It was Peta-Gaye.

She went missing last week, and no one knows where she is. Her father was crying and praying in church yesterday. He said her clothes and shoes are still at his home. She helped him sell red syrup over crushed ice in plastic bags on Saturdays. She would carry them, six at a time. Among the other sellers offering mangoes, tamarind balls, guinep and sour sap, you could hear Peta-Gaye's high pitch voice yelling "Sky juice, sky juice." Peta-Gaye had passed her scholarship exam, just like Lorraine. They both took the sixth-grade scholarship exam in the fifth grade. Some people thought they were sisters.

"You know this girl?" asks one of the policemen dressed in fatigues.

"Yes," says Kundu. He looks up at the policemen, then shades his eyes. "That's Peta-Gaye. She was in my class."

"When did you see her last?" asks the policeman, looking hard at Kundu.

"The last day of school."

"And when was that?"

"Not this past Friday, but the Friday before that."

The policeman takes out a note pad from his shirt pocket. "And what is your name?"

"Kundu."

"Kundu what?"

"Thompson."

"What's your age?"

"I'm eleven"

"Do you know where she is?"

"No."

The officer wipes sweat from his face. "Sure?"

"I don't know."

"You don't know if you're sure, or you don't know where she is?"

"I don't know where she is." Kundu shifts uncomfortably in the hot sun.

"What's wrong with your face? Why are you covering?"

"The sun." Kundu points to the sun.

"Oh, I see. Carry on." The policeman lifts his chin. "Wait, what's that in your hand?"

Kundu opens his palm and shows the crushed dirty dollar bill. "It's money to buy sugar."

"Put that in your pocket. We don't want to come back down here to look for you."

"Ok, sah," Kundu replies.

"Ghost going to jail!" yells a shirtless boy in swim trunks, riding by on his wooden scooter.

There are more people on the road now. They're following the trail of the dump truck that not too long ago passed by. Kundu walks against the current, looking down, staying close to the zinc, brick or wooden walls along the way. He looks back and sees Leon shaking his head and talking to the short policeman, while a growing crowd of agitated people are angrily gesturing at the other policemen.

Kundu knew Peta-Gaye very well. She was Lorraine's best friend. Kundu would take them with him, climbing the tallest gravel and cement pyramid at the dump, to fly kites. Peta-Gaye made her Sky Juice extra sweet with sugar. Kundu loved sugar, though it made his eyes water.

The police handed out flyers before: Sylvia, Doreen and Donna were missing, too. Doreen and Sylvia used to let Kundu join their game of Dandy Shandy. Sylvia would fling the empty juice box at Kundu's feet; she never aimed for his head. Doreen would scoop the box off the gravel and hurl it at a bobbing, skipping and dodging Kundu in the middle. Kundu liked playing with them. They didn't think he was dead or a duppy.

Leon didn't play Dandy Shandy; he didn't like football or cricket either. He would sit and watch. Lorraine would watch and read.

Chapter 5

Sky Juice

Kundu, Lorraine and Leon are walking along the Spanish Town Road Highway. The highway snakes its way through Kingston, piercing four garrisons before it gets to the main food supply district: Coronation Market. The big market buzzes with shouting vendors, quarrels over space, haggling over prices, or passionately negotiating with an Uptown patron. Bustling through the early morning crowd are the nomadic sweet-talking hustlers, aggressively selling socks, glasses and fireworks.

Kundu and Leon are selling peanuts and asham; Madda Tee prepared the bags but did not come to the market today. The boys walk in and around the market making eye contact with possible customers. The sun is dead center in the clear sky, and heat is radiating from skin, polyester and woolen clothes. The scents of fresh onions, callaloo and thyme rush through the nose and into the eyes. Everybody sweats.

Lorraine is selling sky juice the way Peta-Gaye showed her. "Sky juice, sky juice," Lorraine shouts. "Sky juice, red and orange."

"Give me a red one," says a man with a long, twisted gray beard. He's wearing beige suede Clarke's boots, grey polyester tailored pants and beige bush jacket, like Prime Minister Manley.

"You can get two for a dollar." Lorraine stretches out her hand, holding the bags between her fingers.

He gives her a dollar. She puts the money in her pocket and gives him the two bags. He takes the bags but holds on to her hand.

"You want to have lunch with me?" he asks. "Have you ever been in a car?"

"No, mister." Lorraine pulls her hand away. "Do you want two more, sah?"

"Let me buy you a patty, I will buy all of them," said the man. He steps in closer.

Lorraine looks around, pointing her hand at Leon and Kundu. "Can my friends come, too?"

"Asham, peanuts, asham, peanuts," Kundu shouts as he walks over to Lorraine. His neck and shoulders are brown red. His eyes are purple, and he is getting a second glance from every other person. Slowly, the bearded man steps back.

"Next time." The man looks at Kundu again and walks away.

Leon walks up behind Kundu, he only has two of his two dozen bags left.

"You're finished?" Lorraine's eyebrows are raised in disbelief.

"No." Leon frowned. He looks behind with his hands in his pocket. "I just have two left. The thieving boy them from Rema grab them."

"Them probably want the money now, too." Kundu whispers.

Leon looks around and behind himself. "We should walk back home through Tivoli."

Lorraine is selling her last two bags. "Tivoli?" she exclaims.

"That's JLP area," warns Kundu.

"Nobody will know where we come from." Leon is still looking around.

"Him look like duppy." A woman and four children walk by. "Mommy a real duppy dat?" asks the smallest child.

"Come on!" barked the woman. She pulls the child by the arm as he stares at Kundu.

"I'm ready," announces Lorraine, and sticks out her tongue at the child, who was still staring.

Kundu hands Lorraine his remaining asham, and she starts to eat it hungrily. They start walking through the produce stations under the shed. Kundu and Leon are eating the last bag of peanuts as they wade through higglers selling yam, breadfruit, soursop, pumpkin, mango, ackee, scallion and crab.

Chapter 6

Hill and Gully

The garrison territory wars are directed by a local Don, who is directed by a local political counselor, who is directed by a Member of Parliament. Citizens that live in a garrison are compelled to vote as directed. The MP offers protection, food and work opportunities, while enforcing obedience with a small army of 'shottas' or paid-for-hire gunmen, willing to kill upon request.

At first sight, the streets seem quiet, almost abandoned, then suddenly it isn't. The bloody territory wars are between the two political parties that take turns to run the country. The JLP or Jamaica Labor Party, aligns itself with the capitalist ideals of the United States; the PNP or Peoples National Party, models itself as a socialist party with ideals politically aligned with Cuba and Fidel Castro. Colors slapped onto walls in bright red or green claim an area in same way stray dogs often urinate on trees.

Kundu is walking behind Leon and Lorraine along the highway. Cars scream by as the sun begins to set over the stale salty smell of the Caribbean Sea. They counted five walls with fresh green 'JLP' written in cap. Murals of slain area Dons sprinkled with "RIP" adorn the sides of buildings and street signs. A loud Cessna C340 dives from the sky, landing on the single runway of Tinson Pen Airport. Kundu stops and stares as the plane turns around and slowly rolls to a stop.

"You always stopping here to look at planes. Come nuh." Leon stops and puts his hands over his head and takes a deep breath.

Kundu's fingers are gripped to the chain link fence.

"Kundu, come." Lorraine taps him gently on his shoulder.

Another Cessna roars in from the sky and lands on one wheel, then another, and then all three.

"Did you see that?" Kundu points with glee as he walks behind Lorraine. Leon struts ahead of them.

They stop at an overpass for the Sandy Gully. The gully is wide and deep. The waters from the storm are rushing down from the hills and through the gully, like a mindless locomotive. The water is muddy and silent, and carries boxes, tires, branches, bottles and umbrellas.

"Let's go this way." Leon points. Kundu and Lorraine follow him as he walked along the path of the gully. There is a thirty-foot-high goat fence separating the Riverton dump from the Sandy Gully.

"The water is fast," warned Leon. "It's probably a hundred miles per hour." Leon is standing behind the two-foot-high retaining wall.

"I don't think we're supposed to be here," cautions Lorraine.

"If you're afraid, we can go back." Kundu assures her.

She points to a sign. "It says 'Keep Out." The sign also has 'PNP' written with the 'P' turned backwards in fading red.

"There is a hole in the fence." Leon skips over a puddle of mud. "We'll be right next to Trelawney Lane and the Deliverance Church. It's a short cut."

The silent water swells and rushes beneath them. The aerosolized air whips the nostrils, leaving a metallic rusty taste in their mouths. They walked behind each other, looking down at the path for boulders and holes, sea rats and mongoose.

"Look!" shouted Leon, peering at the dirty gully water. "It's a car."

"No, it's a just a door," Kundu says, disappointed. "Maybe the car is coming." The three all turn to look for the rest of the car.

"The police were looking for Peta-Gaye today." Lorraine tracks a mirror floating in the rushing water.

"They asked if I saw her," said Kundu. He turns towards Lorraine, who's standing between him and Leon.

"They asked me, too," said Leon. "Last time I saw her was at the 5th grade show. What's the song she sing again?"

"'Hill and Gully,'" Lorraine says solemnly.

"Peta-Gaye said I shouldn't sing 'cause I make a baby cry." Leon chuckles, then coughs.

"Hill an gully rider." Lorraine is smiling and singing low.

"Hill an gully rider. And then you bend down low,

Hill an gully, and then you dance right round now,

Hill an gully,

Hill an gully rider, Hill an gully.

And if you broke you neck you gone a hell,

Hill an gully,

Hill an gully rider, Hill an gully."

All three are singing and humming the song as they walk along the gully bank. The water is moving faster now as the terrain goes into a descent. They stop at a hole in the fence.

"Kundu, is this the hole?" asks Lorraine, sticking her head through.

"I don't think so. It's supposed to be big." Kundu walks past her.

"No, that's not the hole," Leon confirms.

The shrubs and partially crumbling retainer wall are intermingling at the edge. Kundu grazes his hand along the fence. As he looks back at Lorraine, she does the same. Soon they are all running their fingers against the fence as they cautiously walk along a quickly narrowing path.

"I see something." Kundu slows down and stops. "Who is that?"

Lorraine whispers. "What is he doing?"

"He's chopping wood?" asks Leon nervously.

There is a man with his back turned, swinging a machete vigorously and kicking objects into the gully.

"He's standing in front of the big hole in the fence," says Leon.

"That's not wood." Kundu whispers. "Let's go back."

New clouds had already covered the sun.

Leon turns around and starts to walk with his back against the fence. Lorraine turns and steps on a broken root that forced its way through the wall. She falls but Kundu grabs her arm as both her legs dangle over the gully.

"Ahhh!" Lorraine screams.

Kundu pulls her up and back onto the path.

"Raasclaat!" howls the man. He slaps his machete against the fence and starts to run towards them. There was no light on his face and body; he was like a shadow running without legs.

They start running as close to the fence as they could. Leon is at the small hole that they passed and is squeezing through.

The shadow man with his machete has cleared the narrow path and is coming in faster than the river flowed.

Lorraine and Kundu get to the hole. "Go!" yelled Kundu.

Lorraine goes headfirst and is squeezing to pass through. Kundu jumps into the hole feet first as soon as Lorraine is clear, but his shirt is stuck on a jagged piece of wire. It rips his skin, leaving a bleeding line, and his blood is bright like apples.

"Come, Kundu!" cried Lorraine. He's trying to get loose, but the sharp edge is tangled in his shirt.

"Take it off." Lorraine scampers back to Kundu. She pulls the untangled side of his shirt over his head and Kundu gets up. They both start running up a dump hill shaped like a cone. Leon is halfway up.

"Come on!" shouts Leon. As they reached the top, they could see the yellow crucifix of the Church of Deliverance, shining through the shifting haze of the Riverton City pit fires.

Checking to reassure they were not followed, they descended from the peak to the flats and pass the Deliverance marquee: 'The Lord is my rock, my fortress and my deliverer; my God is my rock, in whom I take refuge, my shield and the horn of my salvation. (2 Samuel 22:2-3).'

Chapter 7

Cornmeal Porridge

"You talk to the police them?" asked Ms. V.

Madda Tee shakes her head from side to side.

"They still looking for that Peta girl. She definitely dead by now," Ms. V continued.

Madda Tee is stirring a charcoal-blackened kerosene container on the fire pit. She double-grips the wooden spoon and swirls it through the corn meal and fragments of chicken back and pigtails.

Madda Tee sighed. "Six pickney gone. Mercy Jesus. A blackheart man thing that." Carefully measuring three spoons of cornmeal stew into a plastic bowl, she gives it to Ms. V.

"Thanks Madda," says Ms. V. "Mi know that mi still owe you some money." She tastes the cornmeal stew with her fingers.

"No worry yuh self. Jesus wi fix everything." Madda Tee sits facing the gate on an empty white plastic tub turned upside down.

"Kundu not here?"

Madda Tee shakes her head. "Kundu is alright. Most people afraid of him anyway. He still don't look people in the face."

Ms. V squats by the fire pit. Madda Tee rolls pages of newspaper and stuffs it into the flames.

"Him soon twelve. Mi no think he's going to have a girlfriend. Them say dundus boys don't like girls," said Ms. V.

"I don't know what you saying. Kundu no gay! If nobody no want him, mi wi give it to him mi self," exclaims Madda Tee.

"Lord have his mercy! A ramp mi a ramp with you," laughs Ms. V.

The yard is dark except for the fire pit and a lamp burning in the fourth house in the yard. The fourth house is made of zinc walls and plywood roof. Leon lives there with his mother. She only comes out at night on her way to work.

"Goodnight, Ms. Darlene," greets Madda Tee.

"'Night," replied Darlene.

"We have a lickle bickle yah fi eat."

Darlene comes into the light from the fire pit.

"Eh eh! Where you going?" Ms. V is leaning backwards.

"No, I'm not hungry." Darlene looks tired. "Give some to Leon, thanks."

"You don't have to worry about that," says Madda Tee. "I'm sitting right here."

Darlene walks gingerly in cowboy boots traversing rocks, gravel, muddy puddles, and silver car rims. She disappears into the darkness.

"Poor thing," says Ms. V, shaking her head.

"Mi can't talk. The Lawd say you can't judge nobody. I would slap food outta hog mouth to feed my pickney. What she do is between she and she God," replies Madda Tee.

Suddenly the thudding of footsteps and muffled voices rushes by the fence, through the gate and into the yard. Kundu and Leon are crouched over, with their hands on their knees.

Madda Tee frowns. "What you running for?"

"Jomo!" pants Kundu

"Them leave the gate open again." Leon is still bent over.

"You mother just gone." Madda Tee gets up slowly. "We have little something." She removes the lid covering the mixed cornmeal stew. Kundu goes into their room, leaving the door open. The light from the fire pit makes a giant shadow of him on the wall. Madda Tee looks over at his shadow, as Kundu and Leon walk towards the fire and sit. Ms. V, Madda Tee, Leon and Kundu slowly eat their bowls of cornmeal stew, sitting around the fire pit.

Chapter 8

Joncrow

"Lorraine, Lorraine," Kundu calls out in a hush. He and Leon are standing outside of Lorraine's zinc and plywood box house, just off the main dirt road. Her Aunt Pet is sitting outside on a backless chair next to the door, who stares incessantly into nothing. Her hair is neatly wrapped with a red handkerchief. She gently rocks back and forth, fingers on her lap, twirling her calico dress.

"Mawning, Miss Pet." Kundu looks down at his feet.

"Yes, mawning, Miss," echoes Leon loudly.

Lorraine pushes the door open and steps outside.

"Mi soon come back, auntie." Lorraine puts her hand on Aunt Pet's slumping shoulder.

The air is ripe with rotten citrus and burnt wood. Trucks came in from the market early in the morning. Stray dogs and people who don't go to church are picking from the latest hill.

"Look pon the joncrow." Leon points to the sky.

"They must see or smell something dead." Kundu shades his hazel eyes to see the giant birds in the sky.

"That's six of them." Lorraine rubs her hands together.

"If it is something dead, I don't want to see it," said Leon. "Tired of seeing dead dogs."

"What if it's not a dog?" Lorraine looks at him, then Kundu.

"It could be a puss or cow head." replied Kundu.

"Suppose it's not a puss or cow head?" said Lorraine.

"It's not Peta," said Kundu firmly.

"I don't know," said Lorraine. They look up at the black scavenger birds slowly diving in and around like atoms to molecules. Their enormous wings open wide as if to embrace death itself and all things that follows life.

"Let's go this way," Kundu points down the lane. "We can take this road and get right under them."

"We're going to be late for church," warned Leon.

"You have time." Kundu looks down at his bleeding right foot.

They walk through and pass people that are picking through a dump of crushed fruits, mis-shaped vegetables, and chopped ground provisions. A team of timid mongrel dogs with protruding ribs sniff and grab unidentifiable food that has almost been crushed into a gruel.

"It's going to be over here," said Kundu, as he points towards an old dump hill.

Lorraine walks towards the hill with determination followed by Kundu and Leon.

"You smell that?" asked Kundu.

Leon sniffs the air. "Something dead."

Lorraine picks up a silver plastic sword that was stuck in an outer layer of mud that surrounds the hill. They all move up the heap, pushing aside drawers, boxes, lampshades, toilet seats, magazines and windshields. A few buzzards have landed and have joined them in the search.

"Move, move, guway!" shouted Lorraine.

Kundu picks up a pot cover and sails it towards the buzzards. They scatter in a flurry, then relocate a few feet away. Lorraine climbs over to where the buzzards were rummaging.

She covers her nose with one hand and moves a pink plastic shower curtain with its white hooks still in place. Kundu stops next to her.

"What?" asked Leon, standing a little further away.

"It's a freezer," called out Kundu.

Lorraine puts down her silver sword and pulls the door. Kundu moves closer and forces his fingers through the rubber seal. As they open the door, Lorraine falls on the side of the heap among empty cans and beer bottles. Kundu stood still and silent. His eyes were purple and fixed.

Leon is standing in the same place. "It's what?"

"A baby," said Lorraine quietly. She gets up and stands next to Kundu, who has not moved. Leon turns away and starts to angle down the heap, avoiding broken Red Stripe beer bottles and sardine cans.

The baby had curled into a circle, its little hands covering its mouth. Dark shadows move across the sky, as hungry buzzards now brazenly land one by one.

"They didn't want him," said Kundu solemnly.

Lorraine frowned a bit. "Him?"

"He has a little teepee."

"Yeah," replied Lorraine, squinting at the dead infant.

"Madda T would take him."

They lower the freezer door.

"What are you doing up there?" A policeman shouts from the bottom of the heap. Leon is standing next to another policeman by a police car. "Come down."

Kundu and Lorraine are angling their steps to slow down their steep descent.

"What's so interesting up there?"

"We were looking for our friend," said Lorraine, replying to the officer.

The policeman looks at Kundu then quickly looks away toward Lorraine. "You're looking for your friend up there?"

"She's missing, sah."

The policeman wiped his brow. "So, you're out here playing Nancy Drew?"

"No, sah," replied Lorraine.

Kundu finally speaks up. "There is a baby up there."

The policeman looks at Kundu then back to Lorraine. "Baby?" His face is now twisted, and eyebrows crimpled in bewilderment.

More buzzards have arrived now. An older buzzard with a red gullet has landed and taken charge. They gather around and on the freezer. The door was shut.

The baby was safer now.

Chapter 9

Blackheart Man

Pastor Beloved walks from side to side on his platform, wiping sweat from his head and face with an embroidered red and white handkerchief.

The four humming ceiling fans whip ferociously in sync, as flies struggle to navigate the thick cantankerous air. The women and men sitting in the choir box have their eyes closed; they are all humming and rocking back and forth.

Pastor Beloved slows his pace, as if searching for the words he wants to say. He steps behind the wooden podium. His oversized black suit is made of crimplene, which was dark and partly wet at the armpits. When he raised both hands up and out, they looked like wings.

Kundu is sitting outside on the wooden steps. Lorraine and Leon are sitting inside on the back bench reserved for latecomers. Peta-Gaye's father is sitting in the front row. His head is bowed as a woman rubs his shoulder while talking into his ear.

"Jehovah Jireh, my provider, His grace is sufficient for me," intones Pastor Beloved. "My Lord shall supply all my needs, according to His riches in glory. He gave His angels charge over me. Jehovah Jireh cares for me." The pastor wipes away a new wave of sweat. "His grace! Is sufficient. His grace. Not your grace, not the Prime Minister's grace. *God's* grace. That's why we're here. To receive God's grace. If you believe in the Word, if you believe in the scriptures, if you believe in the Almighty, you will receive grace."

He pats his face and head with his handkerchief and stares into the nodding murmurs of agreement. A rustling sound of handmade fans from old newspapers and old books fills the pause. "It is sufficient! It is sufficient for me. God is all you need. Let us pray. Almighty Father, we pray that you show some mercy to Brother Griffiths today. As we pray for his beloved daughter, little Peta-Gaye. We pray that she will be found. We pray that you show her grace. We pray for strength and courage for Brother Griffiths. Amen, hallelujah."

A woman dressed in a red gown and red straw hat cried out, "Hallelujah!"

"Hallelujah!" said Pastor Beloved. He waves his hand to the musicia*ns sitting behind the choir.*

"Real, real, real, Christ so real to me," Pastor Beloved sings, with his head thrown back and his arms open wide.

"I love him 'cause he give us a victory.

Many people doubt Him,

but I can't do without Him.

That is why I love him so.

He's so real to me.

A real, a real, a real......"

A flood of djembe drums rushes through the room. Bodies that were slowly rocking back and forth, now stand upright jerking and shaking in place. Musicians sitting behind the choir box stand up with the calabash and the shekere.

The choir joins Pastor Beloved in a crescendo of familiar keys and pitch. Mismatched shoes stomp in time on the varnished floor, matching the drums that have driven the once-dormant crowd into catching the Holy Spirit once again.

Kundu turns his head as a reflection from behind catches his eye. He turns around looking at the top of the dump hill that he, Leon and Lorraine ran down from two nights ago. He squints, then stands up, seeing a shirtless man holding a machete. The man is standing motionless. Kundu turns away.

"*Real, real, real, Christ so real to me,*" the choir and congregants sing.

Kundu crawls towards the door and taps Leon's bare feet.

Leon looks down at Kundu, who points towards the dump hill. Leon crouches down next to Kundu; Lorraine slides over on the bench and joins them by the church door.

"Is what that?" whispers Leon.

"The man from the gully," replied Kundu.

Lorraine squinted her eyes as she looked up the hill. "What is he doing? He's standing there."

"Think he's looking for us?" asked Leon.

Kendu continued to stare at the heap. "Blackheart man."

They all looked at each other, and then back at the top of the dump hill. The man turns around slowly, then disappears on the other side.

"*Real, real, real,*

Christ so real to me,

I love him 'cause he give us a victory," sings Lorraine with the congregation in church.

Leon starts to move his lips but without sound. Kundu simply looks back at the hill.

The congregation is standing with a steady sway from side to side; some with one hand up, others with two palms raised above their heads. Pastor Beloved raises his hand.

"I know some of you not right. You're not ready!" Pastor Beloved shouts.

"Thank you, Jesus," responds a woman holding a baby.

"We don't own these bodies. It's a rental. And just like where you live, when rent is due, the landlord, and we talking about the Heavenly Landlord, we must pay. When the Lord knock on the door will you be ready to pay the rent?"

"Hallelujah! Praise be to God. Oh, Heavenly father. Fi mi Jesus!" came shouts from the congregation.

"I want to know: Will you give your life to the Lord today? Rent is due any day, anytime, anywhere. '*No man knoweth the hour.*' Only those who pay the rent in full, will live with God. You will not know hell, you will not burn, you will not be cast in that infamous pit of hell."

Kundu has moved inside the church next to the bench where Leon and Lorraine are sitting.

"Now let us pray," said Pastor Beloved.

Chapter 10

Junjo

A swarm of onlookers had formed a ring at the intersection of three dirt paths. Junjo is holding a teenaged boy by the front of his pants. Blood from the boy's forehead, nose and lip had flowed onto his chest. Junjo has a Guinness bottle in his right hand. As the boy tries to break away, the crowd swirls with anticipation but remains intact. Junjo is dressed in a black knitted undershirt, white jogging pants and brown lace-less construction boots. He swings his arm and shatters the Guinness bottle on the head and face of the boy, who falls to one knee. Junjo picks him up by the waist of his pants and then grabs him by the throat. More blood is pouring down his eyes and mouth into the dirt.

On the inside of the crowd, a dozen men with handguns tucked in their waists watched sardonically as the boy is lifted off the ground leaving his feet to dangle as if from the gallows. Junjo's dark bluish skin pulsates with sweat and incidental blood. He sneers at the teenaged boy as he pushes him to the ground.

"Lickle batty buoy. You soft!" shouts Junjo. He spits into his hands and rubs away the darkened blood trapped between his fingers. As Junjo walks, the crowd shuffles and looks away. Two teenage shottas raised their guns and fired at the clouds that had gathered to pummel upon the sinners. The circle cringed, then splintered into twos and threes and then into nothing.

Junjo walks deliberately in the middle of the dirt path with his shottas scattered behind him. A dead dog is sprawled on its side by a fence in a pool of blood and dirt. The tire tracks of the ubiquitous dump trucks have carved out walking lanes on both sides of the path. Junjo raises his chin to a pregnant woman, exposing the single gold cap on his front tooth. He passes Madda Tee in her yard, sitting on her white plastic tub. She's peeling yellow yams with a ratchet knife. Junjo passes the gate but turns around and walks through the gate. He waves at the shottas to stay where they are. He spits into his hands and rubs his fingers. Madda Tee continues peeling and does not look up. Her hair is wrapped in off-white cloth and secured by black pins. Her big puffy orange dress covers her knees and feet like a blanket.

"Madda," says Junjo.

Madda Tee continues to peel. There are five pieces of yam completed in a black Dutch pot. The unpeeled yams are next to her on the gravel and dirt. Some are green around the edges; others are blackened with gashes and holes. Madda Tee grips her ratchet tightly and shaves the edges of a green mildewed yam.

"How things?" asks Junjo.

Madda Tee doesn't stop preparing the provisions. "What you want?"

"I should ask you that." Junjo bends his knees slowly and perches like a Joncrow.

"'How things?' What kind of question you asking me? I go market, I sell. I go to church and listen to me pastor. Me look after me grand pickney. You know that already. What you stop here for?" Madda Tee is peeling the yam faster now.

Junjo is trying to catch her eyes, but she is focused on the yam and ratchet.

Junjo turns his head to the side and surveys the shottas with one eye. His silver magnum is exposed at his back. He jerks up and stands over Madda Tee. She continues to peel away the course brown skin of the sickly yam trapped in her shaking hand. Junjo walks away and through the gate. The shottas follow him into a lane off the dirt path.

Chapter 11

Jomo

A dump truck rumbles through the muddy path leading to the newest heap. There was no trail of dust, just black smoke from the exhaust pipes turned towards the clear sky. The driver leaned on his horn as children and stray dogs moved routinely to the side. As the driver made a sharp left turn, so did a small platoon of treasure hunters, armed with crocus bags and plastic buckets. Kundu and Leon are also following the truck, along with its smoke, treasure hunters, dogs and curious children. The truck stops next to a ten-foot-high heap. The driver pulls forward, then reverses towards the heap while raising the bed of the truck. A deluge of bananas, cans, bottles, windows, paper, broken chair parts, and pieces of splintered wood rushed to grow the heap that had started the day before.

Kundu and Leon are picking through the garbage. Leon holds up a piece of bamboo.

"This one?" he asked.

"Yes. We need two more," replies Kundu.

"We can cut this in two." Leon holds up a long bamboo stick. Kundu nods yes, then pulls brown yarn from within the heap.

Dogs are sniffing and pulling at semi-crushed chocho and bags of rancid mackerel. The heap is crowded this morning.

Thirty more pairs of hands are digging through the pile, some working in tandem.

Kundu steps down and pulls the rest of the yarn towards him. He wraps it around his hand. Leon hands him the bamboo sticks.

"We need paper and flour," says Kundu.

"Flour, where?"

"Maybe Lorraine has some." Kundu walks through the late arrivers, with Leon following close behind him. Another truck is arriving followed by another stream of eager faces in tow. Kundu and Leon begin to run through the alleyway, jumping over puddles and misshaped rocks. Kundu runs with his head down, only looking up to turn. They cling to the fence and walls.

They stop at Lorraine's little house, where the door is open. Aunt Pet is holding on to Lorraine's arm as she steps carefully with one foot in front of the other, then flops down onto the backless chair. Lorraine takes a half empty metal mug and pours the root tea on the small fire pit. A puff of white smoke quickly rises and then gets lost into the morning sky.

"Going to market?" asked Lorraine.

Kundu reveals a smile. "Me and Madda Tee going to Causeway."

Lorraine closes the door of a small wooden outhouse and affixes the latch. "I'm going to Peta-Gaye yard."

"Jomo almost bite we last week." Leon pulls his pants around his waist.

"If you don't run, he's not going to bite you." Lorraine rubs her hands and smiles at Kundu.

"What you going there for?" asked Kundu.

"Bags for the sky juice dem." Lorraine steps past him.

Kundu is looking sideways at Aunt Pet. "You have any flour?"

"Flour? No. You going to make dumpling?" laughed Lorraine.

"No, for his kite." replied Leon.

"I know that, thank you please," Lorraine said. She looked at Kundu. "You love kite bad."

"Yeah, when you mix the water and the flour, you make glue." Kundu explained.

"Maybe I will see it at market." Lorraine rubs her knees then elbows.

Aunt Pet moves her lips. The left side of her lip and jaw hangs, exposing her teeth and gums. Her greying eyes are fixed on something far away.

"Auntie, I soon come back." Lorraine covers the pot filled with cornmeal porridge next to the fire pit with a thin piece of charred zinc.

There is a Joncrow perched on the heap across from Aunt Pet. Its giant wings are tucked, as it stares, motionless like the devil's gargoyle counting souls.

"Ok, Aunt Pet," Leon turns to walk away.

"Ok, Aunt Pet. Have a good day," said Kundu.

Lorraine, Kundu and Leon are scampering down the alleyway. A new fence has the letters 'JLP' in bright green crossed out with blood red. A smaller capital 'PNP' was written above. As they approach Peta-Gaye's fenced yard they slow down.

"Jomo is a mad dog. I will wait for you out here." said Leon cautiously.

"He's not going to bother you." Lorraine assures him.

Kundu looks up from his feet. "Maybe because he knows you."

"Maybe he likes her. He doesn't like boys." Leon states.

As they walked closer, they could see that the zinc gate to the yard was closed.

"The gate is closed," whispered Kundu.

"Ok, I'll go in. You can stay here." Lorraine looks back at Kundu and Leon.

She opens the gate and closes it behind her. Leon is standing behind Kundu as they both watch Lorraine walk towards a pale grey brick box-shaped house. The door opens and Jomo rushes out. Peta-Gaye's father steps out of the dark room and into the morning sun. Jomo is jumping and prancing by Lorraine's feet.

"Jomo! Come here." ordered Mr. Griffiths.

Jomo walks back towards him, wagging his tail.

"I was going to market today, and I was wondering if you have any more bags," said Lorraine.

"I'm going to market myself," replied Mr. Griffiths. "Just hold on, I'll get my things and the bags."

He goes back into his house and closes the door. Lorraine walks back towards the fence. Jomo rushes past her and stops at the fence. His brown mane begins to rise as he barks vociferously at Kundu and Leon. They both jump to the middle of the dirt road. A sharp horn blares angrily and they jump back towards the gate. A truck rumbles by them, with the driver's arm and head outside the window.

"Jomo!" called Lorraine.

Jomo looks back at her and begins to pace back and forth.

"Told you he didn't like boys," groaned Leon.

"Mr. Griffiths is going to Market, so I'll go with him," Lorraine said to her friends.

"No Peta?" Kundu shakes his head.

"No," sighs Lorraine.

Chapter 12

Makka Beard

Two dozen new fifth-graders were truant last September. The school nurse and parish doctors would be in school to administer new vaccines and perform basic physical assessments of the students that were present. Six children, including Leon, had the mumps and had to be separated from their class.

Kundu didn't notice the needle going into his arm until it was out, and a Band-Aid was covering the small puncture. He was still thinking about the eye doctor he saw last year at the start of the fifth grade. He sat on the stoop thinking how the doctor spoke without moving his lips. The doctor told Kundu that it was impossible for him to be a pilot because his eyesight was bad. "Pilots must have perfect eyesight, 20/20 to be exact."

The eye doctor offered Kundu an icy mint candy. There was nothing left to say.

Kundu sits on the side of a cylinder in the garbage pile next to the church. He pulls the string wrapped between his fingers gently. His yellow and blue kite bobs up and down, as the wind swoops and thrashes it around. The sun is halfway down. The kite pulls to the right, then to the left. It sails sixty feet in the sky. Small children picking soda bottles and cans watch him. Kundu shifts his stance as he pulls his kite out of an air pocket. The kite is now sailing through the wind like a plane.

This must be what it's like to fly, imagined Kundu.

He pulls the string to his left as the kite pulls to the right. He pulled again but the weight was gone. His string begins to fall and his bajie kite drifts and tumbles away. As it drifts further away, Kundu darts down the side of the pile through the children that were watching. The kite drops behind the thirty-foot fence that separates the dump ground from the Sandy Gully. Kundu runs up the pile towards the fence.

He walks cautiously towards the bottom and sees the hole with his shirt still attached. He pulls his damp torn shirt off the fence and wraps it around his waist. He steps halfway through the hole and stops. Sliding through to the other side, he walks slowly along the narrow muddy path with one hand touching the fence, and the other grazing the short retaining wall along the gully. The water was low and slow. Branches and furniture stuck out like hands in quicksand, slowly submerging in a gentle dance of up and down, up and down. Kundu is walking sideways now, with his back against the fence. He arrives at a widening in the path and sees the kite caught on a rusted bicycle frame; the kite dangles with the slightest wind. Tied to the fence is a blue and grey tarpaulin anchored by two giant boulders.

Kundu peered into the narrow opening of the tarpaulin. It was shaped like a scalene triangle, and blocked the path. Next to the fence was a fire pit with a circle of stones, burned wood and cardboard. Climbing atop the retaining wall, Kundu glances behind with every step. His blotchy feet and legs tremble as his arms are raised above his head as if on a trapeze. He looks up and the kite is still there. He looks behind again, then down. He looks up and the kite is floating away. He freezes. The kite slowly drifts into the air swooshing from side to side, then falls gently into the greying brown flow. It floats peacefully as if coming to its final resting place. The kite turns onto its side, then flips over and slowly disappears.

Kundu turns away, looking down at his feet - but four steps away are two more feet, and staring intensely back at him are two bloodshot eyes that belong to the shirtless man that chased him, Leon and Lorraine. The same man that stood at the top of the tall heap with a machete - was standing before him. His hair was locked and hung several inches past his shoulders. His thick knotted beard and mustache covered his mouth. Old keloid scars are scattered around his chest and arms. His ankle-high khaki pants were secured to his waist with a red, green and yellow belt. The shiny machete was motionless in his left hand.

"Junjo send you?" he asked.

"No, I don't know him," said Kundu cautiously.

"You don't know Junjo!"

"No, not really. I see him." Kundu wipes sweat from his forehead and eyes.

"I see you the other day."

"I go to that church."

"Church?" The machete man sucked his teeth. "Not talking about the church. You and your friends."

A vinyl poster with the face of Michael Manley and the words '*Democratic Socialism Now!*' floats down the gully beneath them.

"We were lost. We think there was a short cut." Kundu said apologetically as he finally exhaled.

Machete Man relaxes a bit. "Mi know you. From you a baby. Madda Tee a grow you."

"Yes." Kundu wipes his sweaty palms on what remained of his torn shirt.

"A me dem call Makka Beard." He walks backward without looking, and steps down from the edge of the wall next to the boulder and tarpaulin. Kundu walks slowly focusing on Makka Beard and the ledge. He gets to the end of the tarpaulin and jumps down from the wall.

"Long time I don't see you." He puts his machete against the fence. "I know Madda Tee. I used to sell things for her a Coronation when I was a youth like you. Which school you go?"

"Denham Town Primary," says Kundu.

"Big JLP area that. Don't make anyone think say you're a comrade. Don't wear anything red. Pure wicked people down there. Even up here, wicked people, murderer, thief, blackheart man. This place yah soon burn, man. All that church, a wicked people that." Makka Beard opens the flap that forms a tent door. There are several plants growing in pots and trays inside. Makka Beard takes out a chair made of brown bamboo.

"Ease yourself." Makka Beard points to the chair. He reaches into his tent and takes out a coconut shell and a ten-inch cut section of a garden hose. He reached in his pocket and retrieves a plastic bag with dried marijuana. As Kundu walks toward the chair, he counts twenty plants under the tarpaulin tent. Makka Beard leans against the retaining wall while stuffing the marijuana into the top of the coconut shell.

"Mi know you mother too, Pifanie. Ms. Pifanie. I did like her, but you know how it go. Nobody want dem daughter to hitch up with Rasta man. Old niegga." He takes a long-inhaled draw from the hose, then lets out a plume of white smoke high above his head. "She still live in Montego Bay?"

Kundu looks down at his feet. "I don't know. She don't talk to me."

"She don't talk to you?" Makka Beard exhales. "She tell you that?"

"No, she never say anything. And she don't come here."

"When the last time you see her?"

"Long time. I don't remember." Kundu gets up from the bamboo chair. "I have to go back through the fence."

"You have you two little friends from the other day?" asks Makka Beard.

"Yes, we going somewhere."

Makka Beard nods. "Alright, man: Shadrach, Meshach and Abednego. Jah Bless."

As Kundu walks along the narrow path, he sees Makka Beard stretched out on the bamboo chair. There, hovering above him, is a giant plume of clouds sitting in the sky. Kundu crawled through the fence and up the pile towards the other side.

He wondered how his mother was after all this time, and why he can't remember her face anymore. When people in the yard ask her what happen to Pifanie, Madda Tee would always say she works in Montego Bay or Ocho Rios.

Madda Tee would get cross and vex when Kundu ask who is his father.

Then Madda Tee would ask if the yard sweep yet.

Chapter 13

36 Chambers

"**W**hy we looking over here? We would have smelled something by now," says Leon, sniffing the air. He is looking between slabs of cement and steel rods. Kundu and Lorraine are looking at opposite ends of the construction pile of debris.

"Him right. We would smell something. The birds would be here, too," agreed Kundu.

They begin to walk along a row of dump piles that draws no interest from the treasure hunters.

Lorraine takes a deep breath as she passes each one.

"What will we do if we find her?" Kundu picks up a can of condensed mild with a tiny hole at the side.

"I don't know." Lorraine covers her nose.

"She baptize?" asked Leon.

"I don't know." Lorraine stops every four steps to smell the air.

The tall industrial filled piles were now joined at the base creating a rocky sea, high above their heads. There is a blue jeep pickup truck slowly moving one hundred yards behind them. Kundu looks around and moves to the side. Leon and Lorraine both follow him.

"Did you go to market yesterday?" asked Lorraine.

"No, he didn't," replied Leon. "He went to the gully and almost get chop up."

Lorraine was surprised. "Gully?"

"Mi kite did blow away. I go look for it."

"And what happen?" Lorraine stops in front of him. Leon kicks a bottle cap while walking.

"The man," replied Kundu.

"With the machete?" Lorraine's eyes grow wide.

"Yes, Makka Beard. Him not bad. We talk."

Lorraine's mouth dropped open. "Same one that chase us?"

"He thought we were there to rob him."

"Then what was he chopping up?"

Kundu shrugged. "I didn't ask him. He's a Rasta man."

"The man almost kill us," she shrieks.

The jeep stops next to them. Four policemen with M16 rifles pointing to the sky are staring at Kundu and Lorraine. Leon stops and picks up the bottle cap.

There is heat rushing from the jeep as the engine rumbles and shakes. The nozzle of the driver's M16 pokes through the side window and rests on the mirror.

"What you doing here?" asked the policeman in the front passenger seat.

He opens his door and walks around towards Lorraine and Kundu. "You!" He points at Leon. "Come over here." He points to an invisible marker in front of his feet. "Tell me something. What you doing over here?"

"Nothing." said Kundu and Lorraine.

"Ok, so you sightseeing. Look yah, man. Every day we find dead man. Three, four, all six sometimes. Some of them your age. Gunshot, no partial. This is election season. JLP a take PNP area, and PNP a take JLP area. Listen, unuh go home. Now!" The policeman walks back around and climbs into the jeep. As the car slowly moves away, the feet of a lifeless man wearing construction boots are hanging from the rear.

"A dead man dat," pronounced Leon.

Kundu turns and starts walking in the opposite direction. "We should hurry up like the policeman say."

"What's the man's name? Makka?" asked Lorraine.

"Makka Beard."

"Did you talk to him too?" Lorraine whispered to Leon.

"No. I didn't see him." Leon kicks another bottle cap.

"He went to Cross Roads," said Kundu

"Went to State Theater," Leon announces.

Lorraine is impressed. "I've never been to a movie."

"A lie you a tell," Leon laughs.

"You don't believe me?"

"My cousin works there. I get in free." Leon pulls up his pants around his waist and ties the string tighter.

"This way faster." Kundu turns into a narrow alley way. "This will go to Standpipe."

They race through a line of zinc fences.

"Which movie you see?" asks Kundu, running behind Leon.

"The new one. 'Thirty-Six Chambers of Shaolin.' It wicked."

"I have to get a pail for water," Lorraine interrupts, and points to the left. "Over here."

They run until the narrow lane ends and a wide clearing along the truck route appears.

Aunt Pet is sitting on her chair looking away towards the sky. Lorraine goes into the house.

"Good afternoon, Aunt Pet." Leon waves at her. She doesn't move or speak.

"Good afternoon, Aunt Pet." Kundu looks down and away at the Joncrow buzzard, crouched atop the steeple-shaped pile across from them.

Aunt Pet stares vacantly away. Lorraine comes out of the house with a yellow bucket.

"We going Standpipe?" Leon whines.

"I have to get water." Lorraines says again.

"Me too," adds Kundu. "I have to get water for Madda Tee."

"Soon come, Aunt Pet." Lorraine puts the bucket on top of her head.

"Yes, Aunt Pet, we soon come," repeat Kundu and Leon in unison.

A woman holding a small crying baby, with two more children walking behind her slowed down to stare at Kundu. The children are naked, except for yellowing nappies and old ripped chemise baby tops. The baby was latched onto its mother's breast. The mother's hair was thick and matted with Vaseline. She looked at Kundu from his head to his bare feet, then pulled the two newly walking children closer to her legs.

"A what show you see?" Lorraine interrupted.

"'Thirty-Six Chambers of Shaolin.' You can learn how to fight if you watch kung fu movie."

"What happen in it?" asked Lorraine.

"A whole heap of things! There is a kung fu guy, and some soldiers beat him up. They fight kung fu better than the guy. The soldiers come into his village and want to take over everything. So, him say no. So them kick him up, and mash up him face. Them beat him up bad. Look like him dead. But him end up outside a shaolin temple. The monk them bring him inside and fix him up. Then they teach him how to fight, shaolin style. He learned thirty-six chambers of style. When he learned the chambers, he turn the baddest, even better than the shotta them."

Leon walks out to the middle of the path and crouches to the ground with his arms spread out.

"I know tiger claw, monkey fist, dragon's paw, snake, crane." Leon is kicking and punching the air. "You have to be fast." Leon is jumping and spinning. "I'm going to train every day."

"I want to learn kung fu." says Lorraine.

"When I finish training, I will show you and Kundu."

"Shaolin temple in Jamaica?" Kundu asks cautiously.

"I training myself. Maybe I can go star in a movie." Leon kicks, then punches the air. Standing with his legs wide apart and his hands on his hips, he pushes his palms out in front of his chest while exhaling slowly.

Kundu looks at him. "What's that?"

"Crane," says Leon, breathing and exhaling deeply.

"That's a bird," said Kundu. "It has a long neck."

Lorraine looked puzzled. "Cranes can fight?"

"I don't know." Leon's spirited kung fu antics continue. "Maybe."

They all start walking in a line close to the fences.

Chapter 14

Shorty

A buzzing crowd of Riverton City parents has gathered around two police cars. The cars were parked across the pathway blocking a dump truck. The driver of the truck was standing on the step of the door, peering through the open window. The police had stopped all traffic while an investigation of a newly discovered body of a young girl was being performed.

Another dump truck arrives and blows its horn. It stops abruptly as its wheels and gears grind loudly. Dust and the smell of hot rubber fills the air. The driver pulls down on his air horn; it bellows impatiently. A policeman walks over to the door of the second truck. He talks to the driver while pointing his finger and resting his other hand on his holster and gun. The crowd grumbles lowly in a beehive chorus of dissatisfaction.

"Dem love hold on to dem gun you see," said a higgler, holding four empty baskets.

"A because dem find one of the girls," called out a man with his right leg amputated twelve inches below his hip. He hobbled closer to the first truck with one crutch while carrying two empty buckets.

"A who dem find?" asked the higgler.

"Me no know. I hear say is the short gyal. Shorty."

The crowd begins to buzz even louder than before.

Madda Tee is sitting on a bucket inside her fence. Kundu, Leon and Lorraine are standing next to her. More people are gathering as another truck stops behind the second.

The policeman with his hand on his holster gets back in his car.

"Shorty dead." Kundu pushes his toes into the mud.

"She dead." Lorraine's shoulders slump.

"Who's she?" asked Madda Tee.

Kundu's toes dig deeper into the mud. "She is in the fourth grade. She about ten."

"Lawd have mercy." Madda Tee waves away an annoying fly. "Only God know what that pickney go through."

The police cars pull away slowly through the crowd. The trucks and treasure hunters follow behind like a somber procession destined to a final resting place.

Madda Tee gets up and hands Kundu the bucket. "Mind yourself," she says, pointing to Lorraine. "You have blackheart man out deh. A little girl them want. A six pickney missing, right? All of dem a girl. If dem find this Shorty girl, dem can find the rest. Poor pickney. A whah dis pon we Father God." She shakes her head as she hands Kundu a crocus bag.

"Hurry up before everything done," urges Madda Tee. Lorraine picks up another crocus bag and Leon picks up another bucket. They all walk out, following the procession through a cloud of diesel engine smoke.

Chapter 15

Madda Tee II

Long before Jamaica's long-awaited independence from Great Britain in 1962, waves of young people crowded the cross-country train to Kingston in search of work. In Kingston, the local bars frequented by fresh factory workers, were playing rock steady and ska music until late in the morning. Everyone in Kingston was from somewhere else.

Madda Tee never got to Kingston until 1970. By the time she got there, she was already fifty years old with two adult children. Her first child was a little girl named Hyacinth. She was born at night on Boxing Day, on Madda Tee's father's farm in Dry Hill Hanover. The baby's father was a tailor from Bog Walk. Everybody who knew him called him Prince. He wore a suit and ascot all the time, even when he was sweating feverishly.

He was shipped to Florida as a farm worker two days after Hyacinth was born. Hyacinth had dark wavy hair and dark coco skin like Madda Tee. Prince was red-boned like his parents, and his hair was brown and coarse. Prince's father grabbed him by the collar and dragged him to the docks. There he paid the ship's captain to take him on board. Madda Tee never saw him again.

Two months after he left, Madda Tee found Hyacinth in her wooden crib, holding a rattle tightly between her little fingers. Her wavy hair, parted at the center, had two pink ribbons with white embroidered edges. Her chubby legs, peppered with mosquito bites, were curled beneath her. She had died in her sleep. She was buried in a little white box on the farm next to Madda Tee's mother, Glorithia Thompson, who had borne twelve children. With the exception of Madda Tee and Gurty, all of her children died before the age of nine.

Glorithia believed that someone had cast a spell on her, and was sure it was obeah. Madda Tee prayed to White Jesus every night after Hyacinth died. She asked graciously for protection. Her pastor declared that no harm shall come to her children. She was free of the obeah, now that she was washed in the mighty blood of the Lamb. The family would be blessed.

The spiritual connection between Madda Tee and her pastor bore a set of twins; a boy and a girl. She named the boy Moses, and the girl Epiphani. No one in Dry Hill knew who the father was. The pastor went back to England and a local pastor was assigned to carry out the teachings of the Church of God.

Madda Tee never went to church as often as before.

As her two children grew, she would harvest and sell green bananas at the market for her father, Big Leaf. He was a proud banana man; up at four every morning, pulling, and lifting, dragging, digging, tying and carrying. Everyone had to look up at his six-foot eleven-inch frame. His fingers were the size of the bananas he grew. Big Leaf wore black rubber boots that stopped right at the knees. His shirt and pants were school-boy khaki, sprinkled with a variety of stains. His deep sunken eyes, surrounded by dark rings, had become jaundiced. He had the sugar, like Glorithia, but now his liver was failing.

Gurty, who had found work and high society in Kingston, returned to Dry Hill to tend to him. She would read to him, change his clothes and rub his feet. When he couldn't speak anymore, he would stare out the window at the banana field. His massive hands were now shaking almost all the time. When Madda Tee, Gurty and the children left the room, heavy crystal-clear water would gather in his tea-cup eyes and overflow into tears down his cheeks.

He was buried next to Glorithia and Hyacinth on a lonesome Tuesday. He was the last of his generation. He had no brothers and sisters, only children to tend to the farm his pappy was proud to call home.

Chapter 16

Dandy Shandy

"It touch you!" pouts Leon.

Lorraine jumps to her left, narrowly missing the milk box stuffed with paper. "No!" she exclaimed.

Kundu catches the milk box and throws it at Lorraine again. Lorraine ducks under the box and Leon catches it off the ground. He lunges, throwing the milk box while grunting strenuously.

Lorraine jumps over the box and turns to face Kundu.

"That's six." says Lorraine.

Kundu swings his arm backwards and throws the milk box at Lorraine's feet. She skips.

"That's seven!" She breathes heavily.

Leon hurls the milk box at Lorraine and it brushes her right arm.

"My go," he says.

There is a teenaged boy writing 'JLP' with bright green paint on the zinc fence across from Madda Tee's yard. Kundu stops playing and holds the milk box over his head with both hands. As the boy paints, his ribs become exposed from beneath his grey undershirt. He has green paint on his hands as well as on his brown gabardine pants. His strokes are big and fast, leaving paint on the dirt and gravel below. He grabs his bucket of paint and walks quickly towards another fence.

Kundu, Lorraine and Leon all stood in silence. Madda Tee is standing on the steps to her zinc roofed single room house.

"All a you come inside."

A beige Ford Cortina slowly follows the boy with the paint as he tags fences along the path.

"But mi no get my turn yet," protested Leon to Kundu and Lorraine.

"Come inside!" Madda Tee takes a step towards them.

"Come." Kundu waves his hand at Leon.

Lorraine and Leon follow Kundu as he hurries past Madda Tee, who walks behind them and closes the door.

"You see the Laborite them a markup the place." said Madda Tee. "They want this area."

She turns two thick bent nails that are fixed into the door and locks them into the cinder block wall. The children all sit in darkness on Kundu's cardboard box bed. Madda Tee sits on her box spring and motions to the children to get lower. The grey wall is cold and damp to the touch. There is the sound of a woman's voice screaming "Woaeeeee, Lawd Jesas!" The scream is getting louder and louder, then fades away. There is silence except for the rapid breathing of the children. Madda Tee sits still in the darkness. A long sliver of muted light forces itself through the bottom of the door.

"Murdah! Jesas Chrise. A kill dem ago kill him," yelled a woman just outside the door.

There are deeper, frantic unidentifiable voices of several men shouting angrily from further away. The voices ring through the single room. Leon wipes tears from his eyes. Kundu lies flat on his stomach and motions for Lorraine and Leon to do the same. They hurriedly lie on opposite sides of Kundu. Madda Tee rolls and slides off her box spring and grunts as she sinks to the uneven floor.

She moves her pee pot closer to the corner, then lays on her side with her left arm under her head. Suddenly a stampede of feet running just outside the door and through the yard shakes the zinc roof. A car blaring its horn rumbles loudly past the yard. There are two explosions not far away. Kundu holds up two fingers, counting the gunfire. Then there came a return of 8 more explosions just outside the yard. Leon holds up seven fingers. Kundu shakes his head and holds up ten fingers.

"I have to go home," whispers Lorraine.

Kundu shakes his head. "Too much shottas out there."

"I have to help Aunt Pet go inside," she replied.

"Look here," said Madda Tee in a hush. "You have to wait. You can't go out there now. You don't hear how much shot a fire? You can't go out there darlin', just hold on. You aunt will be alright. All you can do right now is pray for her. Leon, pray for your mother, too." Madda Tee sits up.

"My mother gone to work."

Madda Tee nods. "Yes, all the more reason to pray, right. Close your eyes."

Lorraine bows her head and closes her eyes. Leon looks over at Lorraine, then clasps his hands and closes his eyes tightly. Kundu looks over at Madda Tee; she nods and he closes his eyes.

Madda Tee rises to her knees and raises her right hand. "Lawd Father God, because of You I have food and shelter over our head. Because of you Father God, we live to see the sun one more day. Oh Father God, you deliver us from the devil. Oh Father God, you save our soul. Watch over us, Father God.

Keep us from the wickedness and the wicked people. Oh Father God, watch over these children, Father God. Protect them. We offer praises in your name, Father God." Madda Tee pauses.

The dull, doughy body of a fully-grown grey croaking lizard crawls slowly up the cinder block wall, its tail dancing from side to side.

Outside, the screams and shouting had stopped. There was no sound except for the children's synchronized breathing. The silence was thick, as if searching for a heartbeat.

"Thank you, Jesus," exhaled Madda Tee.

Chapter 17

Rain a Fall

August is hurricane time. It's the one season that is full of little surprises. Zinc roofs always suffer the indignity of leaks and sometimes being blown away and lost forever. Lucky scavengers quickly claim what they can to sell or simply restore what they lost. The rain and wetness dull the crisp fierce decay of the garbage heaps. The smell of rotting things is less sharp, but for the unique decay of flesh.

A group of men, women and children were gathered by the base of an old mountain heap. A thin policeman is on his radio while sitting in his car; one leg in the car and the other out. Another policeman is standing over a bundle of plastic wrap next to large suitcase. Small children, some in underpants, some with nothing at all, are playing a game amongst themselves.

"Rain a fall breeze a blow, chicken batty outta door," they shout.

A police jeep arrives with two more policemen in the front and two sitting in the open back. They are wearing navy blue uniforms and black helmets. Their pants are tucked into their shiny high-top black boots. They each had an M16 rifle lowered to the ground, as they parted the crowd that had slowly grown.

It was noon. The sun was at the top of the sky, but little drops of rain frizzed through the air. Old tales in Jamaican folklore claim that when the sun shines and rain fall simultaneously, the devil and his wife are fighting.

The children played and squeaked, as the policemen lift the plastic-wrapped body and eased it into the back of the jeep. The police motorcade then moves quietly away, though the narrow lane crowded with gaunt faces.

"Rain a fall, breeze a blow, chicken batty outta door.

"Rain a fall breeze a blow, chicken batty outta door.

"Rain a fall breeze a blow, chicken batty outta door."

The children played.

Chapter 18

Comrade!

Makka Beard drops pieces of wood chips into the fire. His pot, boiling with green bananas, rests on a charred tire rim under the edge of his tarpaulin. There is a smaller metal pan next to the tire rim with steamed callaloo. The Sandy Gully hisses and spits muddy foamed water as it rushes to the sea. Pieces of furniture, cars and doors crash against the wall of the gully bank. It sounds like a desperate mob of hands and feet, begging to be rescued. Makka Beard squats over the boiling pot and stirs it with a wooden spoon.

Eight shottas are walking on top of the retaining wall towards Makka Beard. The young man in front has a baby face, and he's holding a Chopper machine gun by his side. There is a pistol with a brown handle squeezed into his belt under his navel. He's wearing a black and yellow knitted undershirt and tailored brown linen pants. The shottas walking behind him are shirtless. Each man has either a revolver or an AK-47 rifle. Walking behind them on the narrow path next to the retaining wall, are Junjo and two more shottas.

Junjo is wearing a red track suit with red and white stripes. He stands behind Makka Beard, his elongated torso cast a shadow over the boiling pot of green bananas.

"Comrade?" says Junjo.

Makka Beard places another piece of wood in the tire rim fire pit. I and I a Rasta man. "I don't deal in politics. PNP and JLP, Laborite and Comrade, Jah no love that."

He gets up slowly and looks at Junjo, who has a telephone scar that runs along his right cheek from his lower earlobe to his chin. His eyes are wide but blood-shot.

"Makka Beard! You turn big big Rasta man now. You escape from general penitentiary? Or them let you out?" asked Junjo, exposing his gold-capped front tooth.

"I and I man free," says Makka Beard.

"You turn religious man now. You're not the Cimarron Kid anymore? You just smoke you weed all day and talk bout Jah and Selassie I. A bad, bad buoy this you see!" Junjo raises his voice, addressing the shottas standing around them. "Bad man this, cut a hundred people with his ratchet. Him used to be cold blooded man. Now him a rasta man. Site up Jah every day. What about me?"

"You?" asked Makka Beard.

"Yeah. Nuh we out here patrolling the area, keeping you safe so you can grow you weed and cook you Ital stew?"

"The righteous man nuh join wickedness to fight against wickedness. Jah know what is in my heart. Whatever plan Jah have for I is for Jah to know. I just keep to myself and ward off wicked people."

Junjo steps in closer to Makka Beard.

"Don't come cross the fence." Junjo talks close to his ear, and points to the machine gun in the baby-faced shotta's hand. The younger shotta hands Junjo the gun, who Junjo points the gun at Makka Beard, then to the cloudless blue sky and fires.

The gun whistles and cracks, leaving smoke and burnt steel in the air. The gully rumbles in response, as more debris crashes against the wall. Junjo hands the gun back to Baby Face. The shottas standing on the retaining wall of the gully start walking away. Junjo walks to the middle followed by two teenaged shirtless shottas.

Makka Beard watches as they walk in single file through the narrow muddy path, then disappear through the hole in the fence.

Chapter 19

Shadrach, Meshach and Abednego

Kundu is looking down at his feet. There are countless scars and chips off his pallid skin. The darkness from the bottom of his feet has spread to the sides, like a boat's outer hull sinks into oil- contaminated water. He's holding a lace-less white sneaker stained in rust-yellow, as he's carefully digging through a pile.

"I have a slipper you can borrow." Lorraine stands at the base of the pile.

"The other foot must be in here. Most times people throw away both shoes." Kundu is hunched over, searching through mangled, interlocked random pieces.

"He can't wear you slippers, Lorraine. His foot is too big and they not letting him on the bus with slippers," says Leon.

"That's not true," says Kundu. "I can wear slippers." He continues to search the fresh pile for the second foot.

"Here is another shoe." Lorraine holds up a blue sneaker ripped at the heel. She walks over to Kundu. He sinks his right foot into the sneaker. He draws the laces tight. They are still very loose. He puts on the white and yellow stained sneaker and squeezes the tongue into the side.

"New style," nods Lorraine.

"I look like ediot," says Kundu.

"No, it could be a new style," she insists.

Leon is digging for items, too. "I have chiney kung fu shoes, Lorraine has on church shoes and you have new style. A we run things!"

Kundu looks down at him while shading his eyes with the blue ripped sneaker. There is a twitch in his dimples that happens when he smiles.

They walk down the side of the pile and pass the church.

"Which way we going?" asks Lorraine.

Leon points. "Through the fence and around the gully."

Lorraine winces, concerned. "Where the mad man live?"

"He's not mad. He's a Rasta man. Makka Beard him name," Kundu reassures her.

"Makka Beard? What kinda name that?"

"Him have makka in his beard 'cause him don't comb it," Leon interjects.

"We have to walk to Three Miles," says Kundu. "Everything is red over there."

"You ask the Makka Beard man if him know Peta-Gaye?" Lorraine sounds hopeful.

"No." Kundu shakes his head. "Him no bother nobody."

They walk down the garbage hill towards the hole in the fence. Kundu goes through the hole followed by the other two. Kundu looks down the muddy pathway towards Makka Beard's shed, while Leon and Lorraine move quickly in the other direction. Kundu joins them from behind.

The gully is quiet today; no doors or refrigerators crash with clanking sounds. The brown milky water flows silently like a thief, carrying away small, unloved things that no longer have a home. The narrow, short retaining wall guarding the gully is tattooed with green JLP and red PNP. Some were nervously written and others with precise deliberation. Many signs were crossed out and written over, in a frantic tit-for-tat edit that included "suck you mumma."

They are walking and running at the same time, approaching the end of the path leading to the road. Makka Beard steps over the embankment and walks towards them. Leon stops suddenly, and Lorraine crashes into him. Kundu steps from behind them.

Makka Beard has a crocus bag over his shoulder. He looks at Leon and Lorraine, then at Kundu.

"You haunted? What you doing over here?" Makka Beard asked.

"We going to Three Mile," says Kundu.

"Three Mile. Your two friend these?"

Kundu nods his head.

Makka Beard walks by them and raises his chin. "Watch you self, Shadrach, Meshach and Abednego." He turns and walks away.

Lorraine looks back as Kundu steps over the embankment, followed by Leon. Lorraine does the same and walks quickly away from the gully.

Chapter 20

X 77

One hundred thousand tins of Grace Salt Mackerel, and twice as many bags of no-brand flour are delivered and distributed by the ruling Party. The ever-popular freeness, married with job proposals in the public sector, inspires votes and fidelity among thousands living at and below the government's poverty line. The poorest of the poor traded their votes for turn-cornmeal, salt mackerel, dark sugar, cake soap and Dettol.

The honorable Transportation Secretary, who most recently successfully defended himself against a claim of misappropriation, delivered in a stunning announcement during his State of the Country address on Radio Jamaica. He announced the addition of a new bus line, the X77, that would travel from downtown Kingston through Three Mile, Halfway Tree, Hope Gardens and Papine. And for the first time in the history of the world, there would be no charge.

Families with nowhere to go, sat like new tourists gawking out the windows, as the extra-long yellow and black bus meandered through desolate towns and feuding garrisons. The bus moved slowly, like a cruise ship coming into harbor. It stopped at designated intersections, often thick with eager faces of small fidgeting children, stewarding parents, mischievous teenagers, and pickpockets. When loaded, the heart of the bus - with the written capacity of 48 PERSONS SEATED/20 PERSONS STANDING - smelled like hard work, baby powder and mixed perfume. The windows were open, and as it picked up speed between the stops, gusts of smoke-tainted wind would rush over the faces of the children sitting by the window. They were all warned by the conductor to keep their hands and heads inside, or else.

The driver was a thin, light-skinned boyish man who hovered over the giant steering wheel, turning the bus with his whole body. Looking from side to side, he rocks back and forth then side to side in a perpetual tango with a steering wheel that seems destined to kill him. The conductor sat halfway at the midpoint of the bus. She had gathered her hair under a blue cap, leaving unruly strands to escape on the sides. She monitored the bus from front to back, giving a menacing glance at a child whose head had wandered too far outside of the window. The grownups are holding on to the silver hand rails as the bus driver settles into his death match with a terrible disadvantage.

The bus stops at the Three Mile pick up, hurls forward, then lurches backward, ejecting a man with an amputated leg from the rear bench seat. He growls and grunts. Some children laugh as parents and adults shush and tender light slaps to snickering children that are too overwhelmed to contain themselves. The doors of the bus open.

Leon, Lorraine and Kundu enter and walk down the aisle towards the back of the bus. Leon squeezes onto the bench seat next to the window, Lorraine sits next to him, and Kundu sits next to Lorraine and the man with the amputated leg. Almost all the faces in the world had turned to inspect Kundu.

The man next to him was folding the extra material where his leg would have been; the creases in his neck are sweating. So too, are the dimpled fat on his elbows. He's looking out the window like the children, catching the sudden rush of air as it whips throughout the impetuous bus. His one black shoe sparkles as his pant leg rides upward, revealing a sock the color of a Band-Aid. He looks away from the window over at Kundu, then to the front of the bus.

"No mind them," said the man, as the bus lurches forward, moving away from a traffic light. "Where you come from?"

Kundu looks at Lorraine, then back to the man. "Round so," replied Kundu.

"Round so?"

"Round downtown." Lorraine interjects.

"OK. Round so, downtown round. OK!" says the man.

Leon looks over at the man and then out the window. An old woman sitting two seats behind the driver coughs violently, slapping her chest as if to beat out the consumption that had stopped her breathing. The bus rails through an uneven intersection, causing heads to bobble and shimmy.

It comes to a screeching stop next to a buzzing crowd. As the new passengers enter the bus, walking down the aisle, they take quick flashing glances at Kundu. The doors of the bus close and the driver grapples with the sumo steering wheel.

As it inches forward, the voice of a latecomer yells, "Hold on deh, wait!" He's running alongside the giant bus. The old woman begins to cough again and beats her chest, then sticks her head out the window. She spits out the stubborn greying mucus that had been trapped within her large chest, splattering across the face and mouth of the latecomer. There's a concert of murmurs and gasping as the young bus driver shifts into first gear and rocks his frail frame back and forth and side to side.

"Mmmm, Jesas Christ! How she a spit outta window pon everybody," exclaimed the conductor.

The old woman looks back briefly and adjusts her orange crocus bag on the seat next to her. The buoyant bus is now barreling through busy intersections, ignoring the outstretched hands of crowds eagerly awaiting its arrival.

"Bus full!" yelled the conductor to the boy driver. He flashes her an annoyed glance, then slams on the brakes. His forehead and armpits are wet. He blows the horn; it is piercing and annoying, too. The bus crosses over the Halfway Tree intersection, leaving behind single room flats with their bright exaggerated paint, grilled windows and narrow concrete enclosed yards. It was the border between uptown and downtown, between middle class and upper class, between the light-skinned and the darker shade, the curly hair and the steel wool hair.

The bus floats now, as it glides on more even pavements passing Jamaica House, home of the Prime Minister. The house is white, surrounded by neatly-cut grass. It is still, like a photograph, or a dead man.

Prime Minister Michael Manley promised education and self-reliance. The opposition leader, Mr. Edward Seaga, promised jobs and American support. They had a difference of opinion. Mr. Manley attended the London School of Economics and Mr. Seaga attended Harvard in the US. Their opinions created desperate men: mostly young men, bodies riddled with bullets that lay sunken into dirt roads; a result of intellect.

The bus bounces into the heart of uptown and all the eyes peer to the right of the bus as the houses on Beverly Hills come into view. They are imperious; white three- or four-story houses perched on green, lush mountainsides. Leon presses his nose against the glass window. Lorraine crouches down to see through the glass window as Kundu peers over her shoulder. The man with the amputated leg is sleeping. His head is against the glass window, along with his single crutch. He was clutching a green duffle bag with 'Corporal Chapman' printed in black, stretched across the side.

"That's where she lives?" Kundu asked.

"Not on that side," said Lorraine. "You can't see it from here."

Leon is excited. "Dem have pool?"

"Maybe." Lorraine shrugs her shoulders.

"That house look like shaolin temple. Look how it big! And red and white, and it curl up. One person probably live there, right? Him one." Leon swooned.

"We have to get off at the gas station," the girl replied.

Kundu nudged Leon. "You have to ring the bell."

"Not yet," whispered Lorraine. "Wait till we see it first."

"See it deh!" said Kundu, pointing.

Leon reaches for the green strip that runs along the panel of the bus. The annoyed buzzing sound prompts the driver to glare through his rear-view mirror. The man with the amputated leg opens his eyes, reaching into his bag and taking out a small transistor radio. He extends the little antenna and turns it on. Static noise interrupted by spotty voices compete and then settles into a faint melody, then a voice.

"West Indies two hundred and forty-nine for three. Pakistan will have to contend with Mr. Holding after a brilliant first leg," said the announcer.

The bus stops and the three children swiftly walk to the opened rear door. Quick glances follow them onto the street. The doors close and the bus jerks forward then rumbles away, leaving a light grey fog.

Chapter 21

Tappa Narris

Lorraine almost never saw her mother, Marva Walker. Marva was a live-in helper for Mr. Chin, his wife Gogo and their son Butch. Everyone in Beverly Hills Jamaica had at least one helper. The helper would cook breakfast, lunch and dinner, wash laundry, clean the house and make the beds. The gardener would lord over the landscaping, plucking away at dandelions, crabgrass, daisies and forty-legs.

Marva could not see her children on Christmas because Ms. Gogo was receiving guests from Mandeville. Marva didn't entertain her secret thoughts about inviting her children, Millicent and Lorraine, to visit for Christmas. After all, she had heard Ms. Gogo say she 'didn't like to be around so many black people,' on many occasions. Marva missed her children, but she knew better.

Marva had borrowed money from Ms. Gogo to help pay her husband George's fare to New York. George was deep black, with a wide forehead and nose. Ms. Gogo would stand on the balcony looking out when he visited and collected Marva's pay. He left for New York on August 6th, Jamaica's Independence Day from the British Crown. George left their two children with his sister Aunt Pet in Riverton City. He clasped his big, calloused carpenter hands over Marva's. She cried as she burrowed her face into his consoling shoulders. Ms. Gogo stood still atop the third balcony, dressed in her silk robe and headscarf.

They would never see him again. He never wrote to her or Lorraine and Millicent. He never sent a picture. They never got the money to buy clothes, food, school fees, uniforms, or to repay Ms. Gogo as he promised. George traveled to New York to live with Marva's brother Keith. He found his way to New York as a stowaway on a ship called *The Deliverance*.

Marva wrote to him, only to confirm what she had hoped was just insecurity. George had fallen in love with a white woman, and had not been seen for over a year. He had married the blonde woman and probably moved to Pennsylvania. Marva now worked without holidays, occasionally seeing Lorraine and Millicent. They would huddle at the front gate of Ms. Gogo's mansion, and the children would report to Marva about Aunt Pet's stinking toe, the little house and the school report.

As the children left, Marva would stand at the gate watching them walk down the hill. As they walked further away, her pretty smile would slowly make way for tears.

Early one Sunday morning, Ms. Gogo found Marva on the kitchen floor with flour on her hands. There was a roll of fresh dough on the counter, with a warm pot of okra and saltfish on the stove: Marva's heart had stopped.

It was maybe from George or missing holidays with her children. Her long coolie hair was wrapped neatly in a bun. Her grey eyes looked up at the ceiling but said nothing. And so it came to be that Millicent would work in the home of Ms. Gogo. The money Marva gave to George was still her debt. Millicent, now seventeen, would work in her mother's shoes. She would get Mr. Chin's slippers and rub Ms. Gogo's veins that seem to protrude from her pale skin. Lorraine now watched and fed Aunt Pet.

Aunt Pet's trembling hands had begun to fumble buttons and pots of tea. Then suddenly, she stopped speaking. Her stoic gaze would look pass and through everything. She was a hundred miles away all the time.

Chapter 22

Millicent

"How far is this?" asked Leon. He's sweating through his shirt and has his shoes in his hands. He speeds up to get closer to Lorraine and Kundu. "You think they have sugar and water? Maybe them have one lime tree. We can jump pon the tree and mek lemonade." Leon tries to catch his breath as he begins to run. "The ground hot, eeh!" Leon skips to avoid the hot concrete and asphalt.

"Put on you shoes nuh?" Kundu looks back at a jumping Leon, who now looks like he's playing a single game of hopscotch.

"The shoes dem tight! Mi toe a bleed." Leon continues hopping.

"We almost there," says Lorraine. "It's that one right there."

"It bigger than church." Leon pulls up his pants.

"Ten times bigger," breathes Kundu. He squints as his unprotected purple eyes reflect the mid-afternoon sun. They get to the gate and stop.

"Alright, so you have to wait here," Lorraine warns her friends. Kundu sits on the grass next to a ten-foot-high white and yellow concrete wall. Leon flops down next to him and partially puts on his shoes, leaving his dry cracked heel exposed and cushioned by the soft hot grass.

"Remember the sugar and water," Leon whispers.

Lorraine rings a buzzer on the column.

"You ever see her sister?" asked Leon.

Kundu shakes his head. He looks up at the balcony as a shadow moves through the French windows. There is a sound of loose slippers slapping the paved driveway. Millicent comes to the fence and opens the gate. She hugs Lorraine. Millicent was slender, with thin shoulders and coarse hair like her father George. She had her mother's hooked nose and light chocolate skin.

"Who's that?" Millicent asked, looking over at Kundu and Leon.

"My friends."

"Where is Peta?" Millicent asked.

"They can't find her. She missing. Police looking but dem can't find her. Dem find a girl name Shorty, but she dead. Six people, only girls missing. Five now since dem find Shorty. Police think is Blackheart Man."

"These boys go to your school?"

"Yes, that's Kundu and Leon."

"The dundus one live at Madda Tee?"

"Yes. Leon live in the same yard." Lorraine's eyes follow the shadow, now standing on the balcony. Millicent looks back and sees Butch looking at them.

"That's Butch, Ms. Gogo's big son. All his friends call him Chiney Boy Butch. Here, put this in your pocket. That's all I have." Millicent steps outside the gate. She stuffs Lorraine's zippered pocket with crushed five- and ten-dollar bills. "That's twenty dollars. You have to make it stretch." She looks back and turns to close the gate.

Butch is leaning on the railing of the balcony. He's wearing a Hawaiian print shirt and shorts. Millicent continues. "Now that you pass you common entrance, you have to study hard. I don't want nobody take liberty with you. Study, study and turn doctor. Look at you, going to big Immaculate High School for Girls. You going to live there, right?"

"Yes, the scholarship says room and board. I'm going there next month," Lorraine says proudly.

"Millicent, the dog food ready?" calls Ms. Gogo. She's standing on the second balcony below Butch.

"A coming." Millicent yells. She looks at Kundu and Leon pressed up against the wall, hiding from the sun. "Well, at least you have two bodyguards."

"Yes."

"Jeezam peeze, you look like mommy every day," smiled Millicent. "Next time I see you, let me cut your hair."

"Alright." Lorraine bows her head and walks away, as Leon and Kundu both stand and follow her.

Millicent watches them walk down the hill. Leon is limping with uneven steps. Kundu and Lorraine look back at Millicent, then turn away.

Followed slowly by her two bewildered bodyguards, Lorraine held her head high as the three walked in single file down the hill and out of sight. As they reached further down the hill, Millicent buries her face into the inside of her elbow. She walks quickly back into the three-story house, back into the tile floor kitchen where her mother's heart stopped. She leans on the counter as she turns on the goose neck faucet. The water rushes into the sink with a sprinkling of tears. Two hands slide around her waist and hold her hips.

"I have to feed the dog." said Millicent. She wipes her eyes and looks back at Butch.

"Dog a dog. That no have nothing to do with me. Unless me a the dog." said Butch.

"I'm feeding that dog." Millicent points through the grilled kitchen window at the German shepherd.

"Check you later." Butch moves his hands away from her hips and struts out of the kitchen. He looks back for a moment, then walks away.

Millicent looks down at the floor where Ms. Gogo found her mother. She crouches down, with her arms around her knees, staring intently. She could see her mother's eyes, her body lying as when they slept together in one bed; she, Lorraine, Marva and George in the small brick house in Riverton City. It was a happier dirty place.

Every day now, Millicent sees her mother on the tile floor. Her eyes are still pretty, her black ponytail with greying stripes lingering past her neck. Millicent releases a scream that drops off suddenly into silence, her voice buried deep within her belly.

Chapter 23

Horse Mouth

Baby Face is leaning against the unpainted cement wall. He's gripping a green orange tightly while peeling the skin with a brown ratchet knife. He wipes his eyes and face with the back of his hand and continues peeling. The fence is high, almost as tall as the baby-faced shotta. It is the only concrete wall along the narrow lane among zinc and barbed wire fences. Junjo is sitting on the uneven floor in the corner of a zinc roof square house, smoking from the dried inner shell of a coconut. He inhales heavily from the garden hose and then releases a heavy cloud of smoke into the ceiling.

Horse Mouth Lucy shakes a bottle and pours it into a plastic mug. The bottle has a Jay Ray and Nephew Rum sticker. The left-over grey drink froths like fresh spit on hot rocks. She hands the beige plastic mug to Junjo. Horse Mouth Lucy was wrinkled in the face and neck, even as a child. Her eyes are squinty and grey. In the darkness of the room, her skin is radiant like newly painted furniture. She has very slender hips and shoulders; everything about her was small. When she smiled, her lips would part all the way past her ears, exposing a bright, brick-white uninterrupted line of teeth. By ten years old, everyone in her small town of Walkers Wood, called her Horse Mouth.

"Is what in this?" asked Junjo, smelling the mug then turning his head away swiftly.

"Crabgrass and donkey shit," says Lucy.

"Donkey shit?"

"Kiss mi rhaatid, how you a big gunman and you 'fraid so."

"Mi no 'fraid," Junjo replied quickly. "Is what you talking about donkey shit?"

"No, is grass that donkey eat and leave on the ground. It we help you nature stand up." Lucy picks up a spoon from the wash pan, puts it and the Jay Ray and Nephew rum bottle in her black plastic bag. She kneels before Junjo, lighting a match that starts a small circle of fire. She then draws a crucifix with her finger in the dirt.

"This one going to work? I still have the pain in my wood. I don't want drink this and then mi nature stand up and then it pain me," says Junjo.

"Yes, man, this is strong. Drink it before it stop bubble up." She takes a small crocus bag from her apron. The bag jostles and quivers in her hand. She unties the string and shakes out a blue and white ground lizard. It plops in the middle of the circle, then dances around, looking for an opening in the ring of fire. His big desperate eyes glow like magic candles at Christmas. The lizard's gullet is contracting into a nervous twitch, while his tail unknowingly fans the flames destined to consume him.

"Hatt callah buch bun dawg. Cyaanky cyannki. Luos ymm serotser eh tnew ton llahs I drepehs

Ymm sidrol eht. Susej. Hatt callah buch bun dawg," says Lucy.

She raises her fist high and slams it down on the lizard's head. His red blood splatters across the circle as his tail continues to wave.

Junjo throws his head back, gargles the greyish froth and swallows. Lucy picks up the lizard by its crushed head while his tail continues to wave, still unaware that it was dead. She gives it to Junjo. The tail twists and wags like a puppy, happy to see its master come home. Junjo bites into the belly and back, ripping the lizard in half. Lucy extends her hand into the fire. The blood on the bottom of her fist boils into her skin. She closes her eyes, then puts the burned skin and blood in her mouth.

"Nothing can touch you. Nobody!" declared Lucy.

She stands up and watches as Junjo swallows the moving tail. He gets up and walks past Lucy as she wipes her mouth. Junjo opens the plywood door and a bolt of hot sunlight rushes into the room. Lucy turns her head and hisses, stretching her arms out as if to prevent a slap. Junjo walks out and closes the door behind him. She stoops down and collects the sand filled with lizard splatter into her palms. She raises her arms high and pours it over her face.

"You're going to be mine soon. All them virgin can't help you," whispers Lucy.

Junjo is walking close to the fences of the narrow walkway. Baby Face Shotta is following behind him a half step away. As they make their way to the end of the lane, more shottas join the procession. Twelve shottas and Junjo walk out into the main dirt road. They all have revolvers, machetes, and knives tucked into their belts and waists. They are an assortment of tall and short, of young and old, but they all had the empty stare of an animal determined to survive.

Junjo stops at a yard with two purple and yellow brick square houses. He stands across from the house as a young shotta knocks hastily on the zinc door.

A frail old man with wrinkles in his forehead, worn boxer shorts and a tank top opens the door. As he settles into the doorway, a little girl appears and puts her arm around the man's leg.

"Comrade!" barks the baby-faced shotta. "You have to pay rent."

"Mi no have it enuh. Mi no work this week," explains the old man.

A horn blares in the distance as a new dump truck rumbles and shakes the fence, house and shottas. Everyone freezes for a second to see if the truck is near. The truck grumbles and howls as it kicks dust and gravel from its giant tires, belching a dark powdery smoke from exhaust pipes that point to the generally blue clear sky. A team of men, women, children, and stray dogs weave through the dust and trail smoke. The truck bores towards the new dump where Shorty was found. It disappears behind its own cloud of smoke, and so too, the ants of desperation that followed.

Junjo walks across the dirt road, kicking one of three stray mongrel dogs searching for food. Junjo walks up to the old man, then shifts his eyes to the young shotta. The baby-faced shotta steps away from the old man.

"Comrade! You a comrade, right?" Junjo asks. The old man nods yes. Junjo looks down at the little girl standing next to the old man. She's wearing a yellowing one-piece nightie. Her two front teeth are growing in through her dark gums. She looks up at Junjo, who is also looking at her.

"How you think you live here? A we a patrol the street them at night you nuh! If we not out here a patrol, the Laborite them would a tek you house long time. A because a we. You see how much JLP green bout di place? A come them a come enuh! Yeah! You have to let off something today.

'Cause you have a little princess yah, we no just dust you out like fly enuh." Junjo tilts his head.

The old man holds up one finger, then walks away to the back of his single brick room, with the little girl trailing behind him. He emerges without the little girl and hands Junjo a small brown paper bag. Junjo takes it from his unsteady hand. He opens the bag, then stuffs it in his faded denim pants.

"Check you next month."

The shottas spread across the road among its dust, sand, gravel, broken bottles, rocks and sand. The last dump truck left a fresh layer of wet sand along the path. Meandering dogs of inconspicuous breed patrol in platoons of five and seven. Junjo kicks a tailless brown hound in the throat, who screeches and urinates as he zigzags away. He walks into Madda Tee's yard.

She's stirring a Dutch pot with cornmeal, boiled chicken back, and red pepper. Junjo is standing behind her, watching her add salt to the dark pot filled with yellow, white and red mix-up.

"Mawning, comrade," says Junjo.

Madda Tee stops stirring, but starts again. The shottas are crouched, some slumping outside Madda Tee's fence.

He addresses her again. "Comrade, everybody have to let off something enuh. No matter who them is."

The heat from the fire pit burns the air. Madda Tee is wearing one of her calico dresses she found in a bag at the end of a memorable dump. She turns around.

"No call me no comrade. I'm not anybody's comrade. I don't bother with that. After mi carry you and you sister in a mi belly for nine months, mi a comrade," says Madda Tee. "No, uh-uhm, no bother wid it."

She wipes the sweat from her forehead and neck, then stuffs the paisley handcloth down the front of her dress.

Madda Tee puts her hands akimbo, still holding the spoon filled with steaming cornmeal.

"It look like she want you fi touch a button," calls out Baby Face.

Junjo cuts him a snarl that turns him around to face the other side of the street.

"Junjo!" Another shotta standing along the fence shouts. "See some Laborite yah."

Junjo jogs to the wall and looks down the road. Six men wearing mismatched green and black shirts and pants are walking hastily towards them. Junjo jumps over the fence and walks out to the middle of the road. The man in front is waving his sugar cane machete. He's sweating through his green ganzie, adorned with a silver necklace that hangs off his pulsating neck. As he and the others get closer to the shottas, Junjo steps in front and takes a machete from the baby-faced shotta. The men advance, forming an upside-down V with one man lingering further behind.

"A Laborite area this," the man shouts. The shottas take position inside and outside of the fences along the road, including Madda Tee's.

"Don't do anything. Mek him come up here come talk," orders Junjo.

People are gathering at the fences and all around. Madda Tee goes into her square house and shuts the door. The shouting man and Junjo are now in the middle of the street. A light breeze in the middle of the day delivers the rancid odor from this morning's dump of rotten meat.

"Mi know say you have big gun over here, but mi no gunman. Me love the blade. A so God mek it fi stay," yells the man. "A who you? Di don?"

Junjo stares at him and then raises his machete in his right hand.

"You know me?" shouts Junjo. "A blood me drink a morning time. You think you can stop this?" Junjo slaps his chest with the machete. "Not even God can stop this." Junjo points to himself with his left thumb.

"Watch here. Make sure you can defend you big talk. We no want no communism in Jamaica," replies the man, walking towards Junjo.

"You and America can go suck out you mumma bomboclaat." Junjo lunges quickly at the man, striking him with the machete across his right ear. The man swings at Junjo's head and shoulders, narrowly missing his elbow.

"Pussyclaat!" screams the man. Blood streams down the side of his face, around his neck and through his green t-shirt. The man lurches again swinging his machete from left to right like a caretaker clearing an over-grown field. Junjo swings down on his hand, and the man drops his machete and turns around, running back towards the other men that came with him.

Junjo pulls a silver revolver and shoots. The man drops to the street and begins to crawl towards the other men. Four men start to fire from the side of the fences. Junjo jumps over a fence and crouches. The two men that lagged behind begin to run down the street, crouching over and covering their heads. Shots race through the lane and through fences. The shottas' bullets pummel the fences that the four men crouched behind. The two men stagger out and fall, crashing face first in the dirt. Another man runs from behind the fence, but falls to his knees and then his face. Two shottas run over to another gunman behind a fence, who was no longer shooting. They fired six shots, and the gunman was silent.

The man with the machete had slowly and steadily crawled on his belly away from where he fell. The trail of his blood is soaked into dusty, uneven dirt road. Junjo walks out from behind the fence with the machete in hand. All the shottas emerge from behind the fences. They walk casually, each inspecting the tormented bodies of the men that they killed. Smoke from the bullet heat, rises up and out into the sky as if releasing a spirit into heaven or hell.

Junjo walks slowly behind the man whom he chopped in his ear. His blood was a shallow pool. Junjo's yellow construction boots wade nonchalantly through what had flowed from the man's now shaking body. Junjo stands over him, triumphantly.

"You wretch you! Where you mother live? I want tell her say you dead. Mek she bawl and drop a ground like idiot. Where she live? Bout you a Laborite," Junjo snarls.

The man is gasping for breath, his face pressed into the dirt. Sweat and tears meet at the summit of his eyes and nose, then trickles into the pool of his darkened blood. Junjo stands on the man's neck and shoulder. The man's hands are flopping like the tail of the lizard that Junjo swallowed. He hands the machete to Baby Face Shotta, and takes out the brown-handled switchblade knife from his waist.

The shottas are standing around Junjo and the man. Junjo stoops down and squats over his head. He plunges the knife into the mangled ear of the man, whose body twists and shudders. He releases a deep groan and then stops moving.

Chapter 24

Return To Eden

Kundu, Lorraine and Leon slump dejectedly on an infrequently empty X77. This driver moved slowly, and despite having a belly that rubbed the steering wheel, he mastered a slow dance that kept the long bus from gallivanting wildly down the road. Lorraine sat by the window this time. Kundu and Leon secretly watched her as tears stream down her face. The bus makes a stop and one other woman carrying a small baby got up to leave. The baby was sleeping now, but had been fixed on Kundu for the past five minutes before defiantly closing its eyes. Kundu didn't see the baby's stare.

Lorraine was inconsolable.

"You sister you crying for?" asks Kundu. Lorraine lowers her head and wipes her tears. She stares out the window from the rear bench seat. Kundu is sitting next to her and Leon next him.

"She can leave that job," says Leon. "My mother leave her job all the time. She's a manager at Annan Garment Store uptown," Leon shouts proudly over the roar of the bus engine.

"We can ask Ms. Darlene if she can give her a job in the store," added Kundu.

Lorraine shakes her head and wipes her face. "She can't just leave. She work to pay for me," sobs Lorraine. "And now them a force her do something." Lorraine sniffs and wipes her tears franticly.

"You can pray for her on Sunday." Kundu wipes sweat from his head and face.

"I will pray for her, too," Leon interjects.

"What about you, Kundu? You never come inside a church. You coming to pray, too?" asks Lorraine.

"Mi no think God will listen to a Dundus," Kundu replies quietly.

Lorraine turns her head away from the window and looks at Kundu. "No, God mek you. How God no like what him mek?"

Kundu looks down at his feet. "Maybe God mek a mistake."

"No, my mother always used to say all things are as they should be. God no mek mistake."

"Mine you mek God vex," Leon shouts above the bus engine.

"God know everything already, so him no vex." Lorraine swipes tears and sweat from her face.

"Mi hungry bad!" Leon angles his face into the warm breeze rushing through the window. "See mi eating mi fingernail them."

Lorraine and Kundu looks over at him.

"You want some?" Leon grins and stretches out his arm.

"Move and gway." Lorraine waves her hand.

Kundu laughs, standing up and pressing the bell to stop the bus.

The streetlights were all bright yellow as they pushed through the automatic rear doors. The Causeway was busy with cars stopping on the side of the road to buy fruits, callaloo, next day morning paper, and pan-jerk chicken. Vendors would cut a ten-gallon steel drum from top to bottom, creating a grill effect that caressed the scallion, salt, pepper, onion and ginger into the chicken.

Everything on the Causeway after dark was for sale. Madda Tee told Kundu not to sell out there because people will tek him away and go eat him.

Leon scampers across the street followed by Kundu and Lorraine, and they begin walking towards Sandy Gully and the broken fence. There is a woman standing in the shadow of a tree who runs out and begins talking to a man driving a red Ford Capri. There is another van parked in front of the Capri with another woman standing next to the driver's door. Her white skirt is very short and tight around her hips and legs. Several other women are walking about slowly but not to anywhere specific. A blue Mini Minor stops and a woman in acid-washed jeans and red cowboy boots and bra walks over to the Mini Minor.

Leon is inspecting a star apple he found on the street, while Kundu touches Lorraine's shoulder and motions to her to look across the road. She sees Leon's mother getting into the Mini Minor. Kundu looks back at her.

"I think I see dem boys from Rema from di other day. Mek we run," Kundu suddenly claims, and they all start running along the road side until they crossed the gully.

They continue walking along the fence in single file. There are no lights next to the fence, just the sound of water crashing twisted metal and furniture parts against battered walls. They are feeling for the fence with their fingers as they walk along the path.

Kundu's hand finds the hole; they climb through it and up the dump hill. Once at the top, Lorraine stops. Kundu and Leon stand next to her, looking down at the Church of Deliverance. The lights are on for Friday Youth Service. The sky is clear, except for the constellation of pit fires and grey runaway smoke. The stars hang low like ripe oranges just above their heads. Kundu looks down at his mismatched shoes as he steadies himself atop a rotted mattress.

They descend slowly, avoiding pieces of zinc, bottles, wood chips, bricks, and pipes.

They get to the bottom of the pile, and Lorraine walks towards the door of the church.

"You no hungry?" Leon rubs his extended belly.

"I'm going to pray for Millicent one time tonight. You don't have to come, is alright." says Lorraine.

"I'll come." Kundu whispers cautiously. Leon looks at him with his mouth wide open.

Lorraine walks through the open door and sits at the last bench. Leon sits next to her. Kundu is standing on the first step and slowly moves up to the next. Lorraine motions to Leon to move over. Kundu walks through the door and sits next to Lorraine. She's smiling. Kundu looks at her and starts to smile, too. Leon covers his mouth and face, as he bites into the star apple he found in an overflowing garbage bin next to the bus stop. A woman in a feathered hat looks over at Kundu, then nudges the woman sitting next to her. Both of them glare disapprovingly at Kundu. He looks down and then at Lorraine.

"Please stand." says Pastor Beloved. "We are one in the spirit."

"We are one in the Spirit
We are one in the Lord
We are one in the Spirit
We are one in the Lord

And we pray that our unity
Will one day be restored
And they'll know we are Christians by our love
By our love
Yes they'll know we are Christians
By our love."

Chapter 25

The Sin of Twin

Madda Tee is sitting on her box spring bed, mounted atop bricks, and boxes of similar but not perfect height. She rubs her legs in the dark, kneading out the swelling that had engulfed her ankles, calves, and most recently, her knees. She gently inspects the sore that was long overdue to heal, but was stubborn and painful. It was weeping at the edges, as the crust would gather, then fall off like rotten leaves sickened by pestilence. She groaned quietly as she made the familiar rounds to the sixteen sores she now nurses. Kundu sleeps quietly on his cardboard bed perpendicular to Madda Tee. She looks over at Kundu. She could see him sucking his tongue as he did when he was first born.

"Lawd God almighty. Don't mek anything happen to this boy. Him no deserve dis life yah. Father God, I just ask you fi protect him from wickedness, oh God. Protect him mother Pifanie, Father God. Is the one daughter mi have. Oh, White Jesus, you mek mi have two children, Father God. Twin pickney dem. Mi a pray for mi son, oh Father God. Mi know say him heart dark, Father God, mi know say him wicked. But you can save him, Father God."

Madda Tee grunts as she prays and rubs motor grease from a paint can onto her legs and feet. Kundu's hazel and purple eyes pop open and focuses on Madda Tee.

"Mawning, Madda." Kundu sits up slowly.

"Mawning. Look here, you have to go to Standpipe today. Get water and check if any letter come for me," Madda Tee grumbles.

Kundu sits up slowly as if being controlled by an unseen spirit. He stands up in his underwear and puts on his khaki pants issued to him by his school. He picks up a floral shirt he had hung on the two blocks in the corner of the room.

"Yes, Madda." Kundu slings the buttoned shirt over his head.

He slides the latch on the plywood door and opens the room to the prying sun. The sickly rooster in the yard across the dirt path lets out a shy cackle, which then balloons into a raucous declaration. As Kundu steps outside the brick house, he sees Darlene walking nervously in her acid-washed jeans and red boots in her hands. Her face and eye socket were blackened. Blood was crusted around her ear and matted into her disarranged hair. Six of her long fingernails were missing from her hands. She opens her door and closes it behind her. Kundu walks over to her door, but stops after raising his hand to knock. He raises his hand again, but the door opens quickly and Leon emerges.

Kundu is startled. "You want to go to Standpipe?"

"Wait." Leon sticks his head into the darkness of the single room house. "Mommy, I going Standpipe." He closes the door and steps down barefoot into the mud.

"I'm going to practice my Kung Fu today. I'm going to kick like John Liu and Meng Fi," says Leon. He punches the air and kicks above his head. "You see how far my foot go?" Leon is breathing heavily.

Kundu picks up three buckets next to the house. "I bet you could kick something off your own head."

"Yeah, of course. I'm training. Watch this." Leon stands with his feet apart and his clenched fists by his sides. He steps and kicks, then punches the air twice. He turns and jumps in the air kicking as high as he can. He pulls the string holding up his oversized jeans that stop just three inches high of his dry cracked ankles. He picks up a banana-yellow plastic bucket and puts it on his head.

"Mi a real Shaolin monk," says Leon, as he balances the empty bucket on his head while walking next to Kundu.

Kundu stacks one bucket within the other and balances them on his head.

"Now I'm training with you," Kundu claimed.

"You have to learn how to kick, too," asserts Leon. "Or you can be Southern Fist like Meng Fi, and I will be Northern Kicks like John Lui. We can train Lorraine."

"I have to dip my hand in boiling water?" Kundu looks at his hands.

Leon nods. "Yeah, that's how all the master them do it. You have to keep it in the water for ten minutes. Even if it a burn you, you have to stay."

They walk side by side with the yellow buckets balanced on their heads, occasionally reaching up to stop them from tumbling.

A police jeep with two uniformed policemen and one soldier in camouflage drive past them, with a body covered with a blue sheet. The Jeep passes by Standpipe and continues slowly with reverence down the narrow dirt street.

Kundu and Leon each join the undisciplined line of early residents waiting their turn to capture water highjacked from the fenced paper factory only a half mile away.

"Dem find another girl. Dem say she tear up bad bad. Har pum pum mashup," says a man wearing high rubber boots over green pants and a meshed yellow undershirt.

"Mi tell you say a Blackheart man something that," says a short, toothless woman in a black unitard. She holds her grey rusting metal pan against her hip.

"A di girl that used to sell sky juice a di market," says the man in the black rubber boots.

Kundu and Leon held their empty buckets in their hands and listened as the voices poured in about Peta-Gaye. Voices began to call names of the bodies that were found amongst the garbage heap: Sylvia on the top of an old scrap iron pile, Doreen in a refrigerator overlooking the gully bank, and Shorty sprawled on the side of a new dump pile filled with broken bits of rotting furniture. Shorty was found naked beneath the tormented browning bananas and intensely aggressive flies. Peta-Gaye was set atop the highest pile overlooking the Deliverance Church.

Her fingers were disfigured and her eyes wide open. She stared vacantly at the steeple; her naked broken body besieged by the sun.

"Our little beloved Peta-Gaye is transfigured, she is even more beautiful now because she is with God," Pastor Beloved had said. "Suffer the children to come unto me, oh God. I am the way, the light and the salvation. No one cometh to the Father except through me!"

A chorus of 'Hallelujahs' roamed through the pews and tapered off into grunts of affirmations.

The church is hot with body heat. The three white fans whipped around a confusion of powder, dried caked salt and ladies' perfume. Peta-Gaye would be buried by the government at a public cemetery for the destitute or unidentified. Her father sat hunched over holding her book bag in his hands; his shoulders shook as his tears fell between the cracks in the wooden floor.

"Give your life to the Lord, brothers and sisters. You don't know when the hour cometh. You don't know when God is ready for you to sit at his feet. You don't want to miss the train. You need to be ready when it comes!" Pastor Beloved shouted. "Come today and join God's army, be dipped in the holy sanctuary of baptism. Give your life to Jesus today."

Lorraine stands up and walks to the front. Kundu remains attached to the last bench next to the door. Leon is sitting at the edge of the bench in front. He looks back at Kundu as Lorraine is held by Pastor Beloved and dipped into the water.

"Hallelujah!" shouts a woman sitting next to Leon. She fans herself with a yellowing rag as she sways from side to side, humming a melody of no particular song. Peta-Gaye's father suddenly collapses to the ground. Lorraine is wiping away the water from her eyes and nose. Peta-Gaye's father stands up with the help of Pastor Beloved and the girthy woman who had been rubbing his shoulders throughout the service. Lorraine searches for Kundu and Leon after rubbing her eyes. Kundu and Leon look back at her with half smiles and half bewilderment.

Chapter 26

Thames

The narrow dirt roads carved out by heavy elephant-like trucks quickly dries after a tumultuous rain. Mixed gravel, sand and worm rich soil get splattered in every direction, creating a trail of excitement and possibly broken limbs. Fences and small shack rooms shimmer and shake as the goliath trucks force their way between curious half-naked children, some only three and four years old. The trucks come every day except Sunday, the holiest of days, when God frowns mightily at all the disobedient.

A familiar orange truck with a Thames insignia on the hood hurls itself through the path. It jumps and rails through minor rivulets of bath water, urine and feces. This Thames is known for damaged cans of processed meat: Hot dog, bully beef, salt mackerel, butter bean and sardine. The crowd of foragers swells from fifteen to one hundred within three minutes. The driver is the same. He wears a familiar beige straw hat, a sleeveless white ganzy. His rope chain was big enough to go around his neck twice. Teenaged boys jump, lunge and hang on to the back of the truck under the camouflage of thick black smoke. The driver never looks back, even after a scream or thud. On very narrow paths, the truck brushes the zinc fences with its five-foot-high wheels. The rims of the truck protrude with silver spikes, ready to decapitate or disembowel anything that got too close. A lazy pack of mongrel dogs scamper and scatter, as the Thames bulldozes its way through their convention. One dog was left in the path, marked by the truck. His hind legs and hip were covered with tire tracks. He yelped pitifully as he tried desperately to drag himself away to safety, his belly was busted open and pieces of tripe was oozing through. The other busy dogs looked on, helplessly wagging their tails.

The procession of scavengers had swelled to two hundred. The truck turns left up a hill of flattened wood and broken pieces of cement. The Straw Hat driver turns left across the path, stops, then reverses into a medium pile while lifting the truck's bed.

The boys hanging from the back climb to the side as the truck bed lifts high in the air and then tilts to release the load. Cans and bottles crash and clap along with muffled thuds of rubber and plastic.

The eager scavengers narrowly escape the avalanche of fortune delivered by the Thames.

Kundu, Lorraine and Leon arrive just ahead of the dogs. They begin to search out unopened or slightly opened tins. Busy hands and feet furrowed through razor-sharp metal and jagged bottles. Each lucky dig is the difference between sunken bellies with white squall, and something cooked over an open fire. Every day is a battle among the old, the young, the weak, the strong, the unlucky and the less lucky. White Jesus can only answer so many prayers.

The Thames driver slowly eases away, allowing the last of the load to roll out onto the muddy track. He lowers the bed of the truck and puffs its smoke, covering everything like a heavy blanket. The driver and his grumbling truck vanish behind its darkened cloud. Old men and women cough and hack, followed by a ritual of spitting and wheezing. More hands and feet descend to feast on the fortune or pain of slightly opened or damaged cans of food.

Chapter 27

Boat

The Sandy Gully is quiet today. The random thuds of colliding trees and car doors have relented. In its place is the sound of dogs barking in the distance. Persisting in the air is the chalky saturation of bauxite runoff making its way down the mountains of Red Hills.

Makka Beard has a four-gallon pot on the open fire pit. The pot was once used as kerosene container. It's now stripped of its logo and used as Makka Beard's main fire pot. The pot boils ferociously: cornmeal dumplings, yellow yam, green bananas, and dasheens. Dumplings bob, dive and rise to the top of the greying water. Another pot on the side, a small, cast-iron pot is filled with callaloo and okra; it simmers with low boiling water mixed with oil. Makka Beard sits next to the edge of his tarpaulin, smoking from his pipe and coconut shell. He blows a puff of smoke and adds a few pieces of wood to the fire pit. He hears the brush and crackle of the dry leaves along the fence. Kundu, followed by Leon and Lorraine, are walking between the fence and the retaining wall of the gully.

"But wait! A weh you a do yah? Shadrach, Meshach and Abednego," laughs Makka Beard.

"Nothing. Maybe I can find my kite," Kundu replied.

"You lose you kite again?" asked Makka Beard.

"No, the one from before."

"That gone, man. You not seeing that again. A sea that dey," says Makka Beard.

Leon is looking over Kundu's shoulder. Lorraine is standing a few steps away.

"You wah see a likkle boat me a run. The pot ready. If unu hungry just eat," invited Makka Beard.

Leon picks up a Grace Cheese can from the edge of the retaining wall. Makka Beard uses a long wooden spoon to search through the grey boiling water. He fishes out two robust dumplings, then two bananas. He adds the callaloo and okra on the top. Leon sits next to the fence and starts eating with his fingers. Kundu and Lorraine pick up two of several hubcaps on an old water barrel next to the fence and tarpaulin. Makka Beard fills both hubcaps. Lorraine watches Makka Beard move between pots, then sits next to Kundu and Leon.

"Mek we give thanks to Jah fi the food nuh!" says Makka Beard. "Jah I pray thee that you hold the schoolers in you heart. That the wickedness that surround this place, don't inveigle them into iniquity. That they will follow the true and living God Jah Rastafari. Make them know that Zion is their inheritance if they are true in their heart. The Lawd God Jah Rastafari will never abandon them, unless their spirit which is righteous, turns against his laws and carouses with the wicked.

The Lawd God Jah Rastafari will protect the little ones in all his region. Jah, with these words I give thanks unto thee. Jah! With these things I pray thee." Makka Beard inhales deeply and exhales a nimbus cloud from his nose and mouth. Lorraine and Kundu cough in tandem as the heavy cloud drifts in and around them.

"When last you see you mother?" asked Makka Beard.

Kundu holds the dumpling between his fingers and bites deeply. "I don't know." He struggles with the heavy cornmeal dumpling, and looks back at Lorraine and Leon, sitting on the ground close to the fence.

Makka Beard shakes his head. "A long time I don't see her. My little browning that. You mother used to go big dance with me. That a during peace time. Yeah man. Me and she was like bun and cheese, you can't see one without the other. Them just come mash her up. Tell her all kinds of foolishness. I know you from you born. People used to thinks say a you a my boy." He eats a piece of yam dipped in okra oil.

"Blackheart man get her?" asked Lorraine, her eyes wide.

"Blackheart man? What you know about Blackheart man?" Makka Beard takes a small draw from his pipe and spreads the cloud above their heads.

"Them say that Blackheart man grab girls and sometimes boys," says Lorraine.

"Nobody grabbing me," declares Leon. "I know Kung Fu."

Makka Beard laughs. "A you a Bruce Lee."

"No. I'm like Meng Fi. Meng Fi badda than Bruce Lee. Or John Liu, he is Northern Kicks."

"Alright Kung Fu master, easy no!" says Makka Beard.

"Ever see a rolling calf?" Leon asked.

"You mean bull cow weh dead and come back to life?" said Makka Beard, smiling at the boy.

"Rolling calf breathe fire. Them have a long horn that dem jook you with. You would have holes in your belly and chest," insists Leon.

"Her name is Pifanie, right?" Kundu holds the boiled banana in his hand, not listening to Leon's kung fu claims.

"But wait, you mean to tell me that you don't remember her? Hold on, what you telling me, you grandmother don't tell you about you mother?" Makka Beard is surprised and looks into Kundu's eyes. "Ask your grandmother why she runway gone a Ocho Rios and Montego Bay." Makka Beard inhales and exhales a slow cloud that lingers around his face. "A she must tell you that story." He adds pieces of okra to his hubcap plate and starts eating.

Kundu looks down past his food and into the ground. He digs his mud-stained toes into the soft dirt. Smoke from Makka Beard's pipe hovers and surrounds them, then rises into the sky and disappears into a fast-greying, saddened sunset. Lorraine pecks at her okra, then finally swallows it whole. She bends her face as she grasps the last one on her plate. She holds it out to Kundu. His purple eyes are hazel now from the clouds and smoke. He shakes his head no, then digs further into the ground with his toes.

"What's your name again?" Makka Beard points to the girl.

"Lorraine."

"When you move round here?"

"Maybe five years ago," Lorraine chews heavily on a piece of yam.

"Oh, you new." Makka Beard nods his head. "I and I no know your family. Who you mother?"

"Marva. She dead."

"Father?"

"New York, not sure."

"Abednego, your mother a Ms. Darlene. Yeah, mon. Mi know her, too. You born right after him." Makka Beard points to Kundu. "Anybody live here ten years or so, them know me and I know them. This place big but it small still."

"What is Abednego?" Leon is puzzled.

"Him in the Bible. Three people: Shadrach, Meshach and Abednego. Them put them in fire because them no bow."

Lorraine wipes her fingers in the crabgrass and shrubs that push through the fence. Makka Beard nods his head and watches the three of them as they feverishly eat, their eyes focused on the hubcap safely tucked in their laps.

Chapter 28

Blood Oath

After Big Leaf died, Madda Tee knew she would have to leave the family farm. A nice light-skinned man sat in the living room and explained how Big Leaf sold part of the deed to the house, how he had an outstanding debt that was one year past due. He was kind enough to let her and her two children stay there for another thirty days.

Moses and Epifanie pressed their ears against the door as the nice man explained that the farm was sold, that the graves in the back of the house would be dug out or covered with cement. Madda Tee was quiet. Hyacinth, Glorithia and now Big Leaf would suffer another family embarrassment. Epifanie would sit next to Hyacinth's headstone and tell her what the sky looked like. She would describe the clouds, the sound of the birds, even the subtle moo of the cow. Epifanie would tell her she was proud to have a big sister in heaven. There were no pictures of Hyacinth, just baby clothes, hair clips and the rattle they found in her hand at the end. Her moments with Hyacinth were the only moments away from Moses.

Epifanie and Moses walked through Dry Hill with each other. They were casually called 'Black and White Chocolate' by everyone in the small town. Moses' skin was dark and almost blue in the summer months. His twin sister was golden brown and would turn red to the touch. If Epifanie was sick, so was Moses. When Epifanie grew breast and started her cycle, Moses would curl up next to her in bed and feel the knots and cramps too. They would stare into each other's eyes and try to read the other's mind. As they grew, they developed more questions. *Who was their father? Why were their skins so different? Is the Blackheart man real?*

Madda Tee explained that their father was a white man and that he might be dead by now. She told them that bad-mind people forced him to leave Jamaica and that he can't come back.

Old people in Dry Hill claimed that Madda Tee breed for two men at the same time, one white and one black. "She a dutty gyal," they say.

Moses would fight and spit on children that repeated what the grown folks whispered. He hurled a fist-sized rock at a boy who declared Moses' father was Satan and Epifanie's father was White Jesus, only she didn't have the blue eyes. Epifanie never got into fights, but inside of her lips were always red and bloody.

With two weeks to go before the nice man in the suit would come knocking, Madda Tee tells Moses and Epifanie that they are moving to Kingston to live with her sister Gurty. She told them that the village of Dry Hill was suddenly being savaged by a Blackheart man. No child was safe, especially young girls. He hunted for virgin girls, according to the elderly men and women. The blood from a virgin girl can cure his nasty wood disease, they claimed. The Blackheart man would know who is a virgin and who is not by just looking at how they walked.

Moses read Epifanie's mind and made a plan to save her from the Blackheart man. As they did when Epifanie had cramps, they cradled in the creaking old single bed. They lived in the room that Gurty abandoned after Big Leaf's death. The floor was a dull plywood neatly riveted together. It glowed from the Sol Polish that Big Leaf insisted Gurty and Madda Tee mop the floor with every morning.

The house stood atop platforms that would let the rainwater run its course to the river down the hill. It had three bedrooms just big enough to hold a single bed and a small side table. There was a large living room with an exposed mahogany wood wall. The two large windows facing the front yard were covered by white crochet curtains. They stood stiff with starch and bleach, never letting the wind blow or butterfly bats in the house. There was a white couch covered in crinkling plastic. The couch itself was untouched, unsoiled and never moved. It stood alone in the center of the room like a display seen at a museum, or a body being revered at a wake. Off to the side is a square transistor radio dedicated to cricket matches and Sunday devotions on Radio Jamaica. It was Big Leaf's prize possession. For fear and suspicion, it remained untouched by even Moses.

He too thought Big Leaf was still there in some way. The outhouse was just twenty feet from the back door. Attached to the house is a wooden shower shed with a water tank on the top. From the veranda, you can see the top of banana trees, houses and even the town center below.

Rain pitter-pattered on the V-shaped roof, then unleashed a cascade of bullet-like drops that echoed through the house and into the room where Moses and Epifanie lay. A rolling rock of thunder shakes then falls into silence, leaving the rapid raindrops to play an angry tune, fast and fierce as if emptying the bowels of the sky. They are one atop the other. Lightning painted itself across the sky as thunder rolls just above the house. It shook the foundation of Big Leaf's house, high on the top of Dry Hill Hanover.

Chapter 29

Tribal War

A heavy Leyland truck burrows through the narrow lane, unsettling the smell of rust, rotting fish, kerosene and burned wood. It shakes the concrete shacks, leaving the zinc roofs to chatter and screech among themselves as if sounding an alarm. The engine roars as it flops into shallow puddles, grazing the bog wire fences that lined the path to the freshest dump site.

A mob of children follow the truck, some adorned in torn or ripped shoes, but most were barefoot. Others were openly naked, or wore nothing more than the stained, off-white underwear found in a dump pile or handed down from a parent. The adults in tow carried their customary crocus bags to carry the sunbaked bounty. They all avoid sharp-edged rocks, broken bottles, open cans of tomato sauce, mackerel and other escapees from the truck.

They galloped into the residual smoke, willingly choking for pieces of molded bread, used furniture, cracked televisions, plates, eyeglasses and old clothes.

Kundu walks closely against the fence opposite the flow of the mob. He looks down at his bare feet as he steps over pieces of zinc and splintered bottles. The dust and stench from the truck is busy in the air like bees working around a hive. Kundu has a crocus bag over his shoulder. Sweat rolls down from his red hair onto his face and ears. There is a dozen or more people at Standpipe waiting their turn to fill their buckets and pans. Kundu walked hurriedly towards the causeway that led to downtown Kingston or to Ocho Rios. He walked along the highway path looking at the ground, as cars and trucks raced in an endless parade of a hurry-up drill. Kundu walks faster down Marcus Garvey Highway until he gets to Madda Tee, Ms. V, Leon and Lorraine, all selling small items at a traffic light.

There is an icebox, a mat and two chairs. Madda Tee and Ms. V are on the plastic chairs overlooking the mat displaying star apple, guinep, sweet sap, sugar cane and peanuts. Lorraine and Leon are walking between cars stopped at the traffic light.

"Sky juice," Lorraine says, as she walks by the cars. Leon holds his bags of red and yellow sky juice without saying anything. He walks by the cars, looking into the windows. The light changes from red to green, and Lorraine and Leon hurry to the sidewalk intersection. Lorraine opens the icebox and takes a purple sky juice. The clear plastic bag starts to sweat immediately. Lorraine learned how to make sky juice sweet with granulated sugar and Kool-Aid. Kundu unpacks his crocus bag of June plums. He found them in a dump truck that unloaded the day before.

It was the same dump where Shorty was found. Her body was naked and punctured with cuts all over her face and pum pum, said the police.

The plums were in various condition, some bruised, some over-ripe, some green and a few possessed with worms. Kundu picked out the wormy ones, threw them into the road, and would watch them get crushed under the tires in a private game only he played in his head.

Leon opens the icebox and takes out a red frozen bag shaped like a triangle. He holds them above his head and walks out among the cars stopped at the light. "Suck-suck," he yells. A car window opens and a hand holding a dollar bill calls Leon, who scampers over to the car. Another pickup truck waves to Lorraine and she walks over to the window and gives the driver a sky juice and gets a dollar. Another car moves slowly towards the curb. The passenger leans out the window and surveys the mat in front of Madda Tee and Ms. V.

The yellow Cartina stops in front of Madda Tee as the passenger eases back into the car. "Unu a comrade or labor?" the passenger asked. The driver is waving for Lorraine to come to the car.

"No, a sell we a sell. We can't eat labor or comrade. Buy something nuh?" Ms. V smiles at the driver.

Lorraine walks over to the driver and offers a choice of purple, red or yellow sky juice. The passenger digs into his waist, then holds a revolver upright. Madda Tee struggles to get up. Kundu walks over to her, and Madda finally stands with his help. The driver gives Lorraine a dollar and takes the purple sky juice. He has wavy hair and a goatee; his skin is light with blots of darker freckles. Kundu is looking down into the car; his purple eyes are fixed.

"Look at the duppy," says the driver to his passenger. "If you kill one, dem tek set pon you in a you sleep. Yeah man. Dem wi kill you in you sleep, too." He spoke softly.

The passenger puts the revolver back in his waist.

"Mek we buy some guinep from you," says the driver.

Kundu picks up a grouping of ripe guineps and walks over to the passenger door and hands it to the passenger. He bends his knees and looks directly at the driver. His purple eyes are bright from the sun. The passenger leans back in his seat, then hands Kundu a dollar in exchange for the guineps.

"Watch unu self," said the passenger. Kundu steps back and hands Madda Tee the dollar.

Ms. V picks up a June plum and holds it out towards the car. "You want a plum too?" she asked.

The car slowly drives away.

"Suck-suck," shouts Leon from across the street.

"Sky juice," says Lorraine to a woman stopped at the light. The car with the two men disappears in the busy intersection.

Madda Tee hands Ms. V a star apple. "Might as well eat this."

Ms. V looks up to the sky. "Lawd a mercy. A wha dis pon we Father God."

Chapter 30

The Digging

The clear blue sky with drifting with feathery cotton clouds, peppered with the angular silhouette of hungry Joncrow birds. The scavengers have found a place where decaying flesh arouses their appetite. They hover, then dive with open wings like fighter planes delivering a blow to bunkers hidden in swamps.

The police have taken down the flyers of the girls that were found, leaving only three now. The parents of a set of twins, Trudy and Doreen, were called to a dump site far into Riverton City. As they walked towards the dump, a growing flock of residents gathered behind them, mumbling incoherently in lock step. Trudy and Doreen's parents held hands and walked reluctantly through the small lanes away from the busy trucks and stray dogs. The dump was not high, only twenty feet to the tip.

Four policemen were there: two sitting in a doorless jeep, and another two standing on top of the pile, moving boxes and pushing tires and cabinet doors to the bottom. The back of the jeep was covered with a blue tarpaulin. The twins had been missing for two weeks.

Their mother wailed and groaned all throughout Pastor Beloved's sermon last Sunday, who had prayed for the twins and their parents. "Riverton City is like the Garden of Gethsemane," he said, and that "the congregation is suffering through the sin of the world, in order to redeem mankind from eternal damnation."

Both parents were coaxed to step forward to see what lay under the tarpaulin. As they got closer, the policeman sitting in the passenger side popped up and stood at the open tail gate of the jeep. The mumbling crowd that gathered huddled closer for the inspection and confirmation of the rumor that had spread since early morning. The second policeman on the driver's side oozed out of his seat, his back and belly narrowly escaping the door as he lifted himself out of the car. He pulled the tarpaulin away. A stream of hands collectively covers unprotected noses. The twins' mother screams and rails as their father attempts to arrest her twisting body and punching arms. The mumble from the onlookers swells quickly into a chorus of yelps, grunts and 'Jesus!' The twins lay together, fixed, side by side wearing nothing except for a bra on one of them.

Joncrow had already taken the eyes of one and dug into the nose of the other.

The crowd shifts and bends as the two policemen standing atop the pile descend and walk through the crowd and stand at the tailgate of the jeep.

The family had moved to Riverton City only two months ago. They lived in Tivoli Gardens. Their mother was a seamstress at Garmex, a Chinese-owned factory but got laid off after the company found cheaper labor. Their father worked as a groundskeeper at the Tivoli Gardens Comprehensive High School, until he was accused of being an informer for the PNP by a friend that owed him five dollars.

The family hurried out of their one-bedroom government house after seven shots were fired into the walls while they were sleeping. Trudy and Doreen both sang in the church choir. Their father would smile as they performed solos and duets. Like Lorraine, they would transition to the top-ranked Immaculate Conception High School for Girls in the coming term. The portly policeman re-covers the twins and pulls the parents aside. The crowd huddles in even closer, along with flies and the dry, thick boiling heat from the mid-sky sun.

The Joncrow birds are flying lower and unbothered by the human siege. Two birds land atop the pile and survey the crowd. One fly-hops to the top of a rusted chandelier, searching out the rotted flesh that summoned him. He lords above the swelling heat and chatter, his beak and head swivels in a quizzical dance, his eyes focused on the nutrients covered below. The feet of Trudy and Doreen are pushing through the end of the tarp and blanket. Their lifeless hands are also protruding through the sides of the tarp. Their hands are closed, like when they held the strings of Kundu's kite. They would take turns. Trudy tried to hold on to the kite the longest, Doreen would call her greedy and wicked, in jest.

Like Kundu, they knew they were an anomaly.

Chapter 31

Police and Thief

The narrow lanes of Riverton City are covered like a canvass with dueling green and red paint. The Peoples National Party favors an orange-like red. It's never exact: each painter finds something that feels close. The party's slogan of *Forward Evah, Backward Neva,* covers Madda Tee's rusted zinc fence. The red marks mean the area is protected by the PNP. The yard directly across from Madda Tee's has red paint covered with slaps and dabs of green paint. The Jamaica Labour Party plastered its slogan *Deliverance is Near* on metal, concrete, and wood surfaces. The paint would appear like magic at dawn, often smudged and wet from recency. The hands of careless children left palm prints in red and green along a trail as they scurried back home.

Kundu sits on the step of their brick house, scrubbing his oversized grey polyester pants in an old orange plastic bucket. Madda Tee hangs her bed sheet and white frocks on a clothesline made from fishing wire. She secures them with clothes pin, then beats the stubborn water off with her thick calloused hands. The lane is quiet. The first truck has not passed yet. Dogs howl in the distance. Grey smoke from Madda Tee's fire pit rises slowly from under a Dutch pot of cornmeal porridge.

A squad of policemen dressed in navy blue uniforms, black helmets and black combat boots, suddenly appear at the zinc fence. They all have machine guns as well as a side arm and one extra clip affixed to their belts. One policeman pushes the gate open and walks up to Madda Tee. He inspects her from head to toe. She's wearing a green floral frock that covers her blackened knees. Kundu sits motionless in his faded brown shorts. Madda Tee had to use pins and thread to make them fit.

"Junjo live here?" asked the policeman. He was tall and thin, but you could see his muscles fighting to escape the confinement of his vest.

"Him don't live here," replied Madda Tee.

"You sure? Somebody say them see him over here."

"Yes. Is just me and my grandson live here."

"Where him live?"

"I don't know where him live," stated Madda Tee plainly.

"You don't know where him live?" The policeman tilts his head, then looks over towards the gate where the other policemen are waiting.

"Mi no nobody informer. Look here, ask one a dem buoy outside. I don't know anything."

"You know Junjo?" says the policeman, turning to Kundu.

"No sah, I don't know him," Kundu replied, his purple eyes darting over at Madda Tee.

"Constable!" shouted another policeman standing by the fence. He walks in and whispers in the ear of the policeman in front of Madda Tee. They both walk away and through the gate. Four more policemen arrive in jeeps and jump out hurriedly. They all start walking down a narrow lane where the one-room shacks are created from zinc and barbed wire. The pathway is sloppy with brown mud, dog and sometimes human feces, worshiped by flies. Kundu stands at the beginning of the path and watch as the policemen file through the shoulder-wide maze then turn out of sight. Kundu follows behind them, stopping at each corner and looking before moving to the next one.

They stop in front of a house, then disperse around the perimeter. The machine guns that were held casually were now gripped with both hands across the torso. Junjo appears from the house and walks towards the Police Constable. He lifts up his white shirt, then raises his arms and turns around. The constable walks over to him and raises his hand. The other policemen loosen their grip on the machine guns they held close to their bodies. Kundu inches closer, then settles behind a drum left there to collect rainwater. In it, dead adult roaches were floating leisurely from edge to edge. The water was used for cooking or sometimes bathing little children before going off to school or church.

"Constable." Junjo walks up and stops.

"Well, I hearing some things." The Constable adjusts his utility belt.

"You hear things. From who?"

"Don't matter. The thing is, you suppose to keep down here under control."

"It under control." Junjo stares at the constable.

"How it under control? Didn't you have a big shootout two days ago?"

"Somebody tell you that I shoot somebody?"

"A man was beaten and shot to death." The officer moves closer. "As a matter of fact, several persons were killed or wounded in the commotion."

"I want to know who tell you I shoot somebody."

The constable scoffs. "That is not your biggest problem. The man that you shot or the man that was shot. You know him? A Trinity brother that." The Constable looks behind and to the side at the other policemen.

"Trinity. Him have gun. Me have gun. Mek him come. Him dead like yaws if him come yah."

"If? A no if! Him coming. My informer tell me say them get one hundred and fifty chopper machine guns a wharf the other day. Come them coming to burn this place down and take it over."

"Them not coming down here." Junjo cranes and rolls his neck.

"This a PNP territory. Your MP say to keep it quiet until after the election."

"So, what we supposed to do if dem come down here. You no see the sign pon the wall? Nobody is coming down here to take over. If a guy come down here a wear green, him dead!"

"Listen man, don't start nothing," insists the officer. "Wait for the word from the MP. I will tell you when to move."

Junjo shakes his head. "Tell the MP say a we a patrol and we need some more tings them, like M16 or Bushmaster."

"Look here, just remember a who feed you."

"And when dog hungry, him no care a who fa hand him bite."

The Constable looks hard at Junjo. "Watch here, me have to answer to somebody, you have to answer to me. You understand."

"Well, a so it go. What you come down here for anyway. We know say you no care bout the dutty Laborite boy."

"How much you collect?"

"Collect from who?" Junjo's eyes look away from the constable.

The officer kissed his teeth. "Look man, the money you collect from the people over here. You have to share that."

"Thief no like see thief with long bag, right? Is just a little small change still."

"Whether is big or small change, I expect to get something. Me and my unit coming back next week. We expect to see a few Nannies in our pockets. You understand, right?" The constable steps back away from Junjo, who stands motionless but raises his chin as the constable steps though the gate. His squad follows behind him in a single line.

Kundu crouches behind a loose zinc fence into an unkempt yard. As the policemen file out of the shoulder-wide alley, shottas emerge from rooftops and holes in loose fences, unnoticed by the red-eyed policemen.

Baby Face Shotta walks into the yard where Junjo is standing. He hands Junjo a lighter. Junjo brings a small spliff to his mouth and lights it.

"Money the boy want?" asks Baby Face Shotta.

Junjo inhales then releases a puff of smoke that slowly disappears into the air above them. "The Laborite dem a come." Junjo exhales. "And a them police boy a go let them in."

Kundu follows the last policeman into the main path, stepping over deep tire tracks carved out of mud. The squad of policemen jump into their doorless jeeps and eases slowly away. Kundu walks through the gate where Madda Tee sits scrubbing her skirt with a blue square of carbolic soap. The rinse pan is blackened with water and blue suds. She continues to scrub but glances over at Kundu, who's still watching the police drive slowly away from the yard.

"Don't mind people business you know. What would happen if them start firing shots?" asked Madda Tee. "I don't know why you have to see everything."

Chapter 32

Radio Jamaica

The diehard cricket men in Riverton City huddle eagerly next to someone with a battery-operated transistor radio. They stood as statues, then explode with disappointment or jubilation. This year, the West Indies team faced the feared team from Pakistan. Imran Khan was unstoppable or simply the devil, in the opinion of most cricket lovers. The matches were being played in Trinidad, and all the islands in the West Indies were gripped with fear and dread. Pakistan had the best bowlers, the best batsmen and the best fielders of any nation. There was a report that a man in Trinidad suffered a heart attack, but was too distraught to respond to medical treatment and opted to die.

Cricket matches were partly a respite for shanty towns like Riverton City. While the match played, the lanes remained quiet as most people, including women, would sit in close proximity or earshot of Radio Jamaica. The matches were long, sometimes three days.

Children, though generally aware of this local god, maintained their skipping games: Dandy Shandy, Stuckey, 1-2-3-Red Light, Marble, and Catch.

Kundu, Lorraine and Leon are at the top of the dump pile overlooking the church. Kundu is flying his second kite of the month. This time he uses fishing wires to hold the frame together and tethering for control. The kite is white. It bobs up and down, then side-ways like a bird observing people and traffic. Kundu wraps the fishing line around Lorraine's hand and then moves to the top of the pile. The kite dances some more, bobbing and diving, then pulls away a little higher.

"You flying it high!" Kundu is elated.

"It's like it's taking me away." Lorraine pulls the kite closer.

"Hold on tight, don't let go."

"I'm not letting go." The kite pulls Lorraine forward and off the top of the pile.

"How many kites you lost already?" asked Leon.

"Two."

Lorraine calls out to Kundu. "Here, take this back before it turn to three."

Kundu steps up and wraps the wire around his hand.

"You love kite bad." Leon contorts his face.

Kundu shifts his hand to his right and the kite dives to the right and then left. He loosens the wire and the kite goes higher and further away.

"Maybe I can build a big kite. I can probably ride it," says Kundu. "I can go wherever I want. America, England, Mexico, Cuba, maybe Pakistan."

Leon recoils. "Pakistan? You would go Pakistan? Just coolie people there."

Kundu gently tugs the wire to his left. The kite dives towards him then floats backwards to where it was.

"You float like an angel probably." Lorraine picks up a pink infant booty stuck to an open Spam tin can. "The pastor said that Peta-Gaye is floating, too. She can see everything. She's probably flying with the kite. She has angel wings, but you can't see her. You can't see angels unless you're one of them."

Lorraine holds the pink booty in her hand and gazes at the kites living in the sky. She smiles with tears running down her face, and wipes them away quickly.

Leon is sitting on the side of the pile, struggling to lace his recently found shoes with fishing wire. "Even if I turn into an angel, I still want to be the baddest angel. Kung Fu angel."

"Angel don't fight." Kundu is holding the kite steady above their heads. "Angel a God things. Them no fight."

"I'm going to be a doctor. I'm going to Immaculate, then I'm going to the University. I want to be a children doctor. Lorraine tries to use the right word. "Pediatrician! Yes, a pediatrician. Me and Millicent going to live in Beverly Hills when I have the money." Lorraine watches the kite and imagines each of them like angels. "I'm going to pay Miss Gogo for Millicent."

Lorraine helps Leon to his feet.

"Sister?" asked Kundu. He moves his hand into a circle and the kite spins in the air then pecks at the wind.

"Yes."

"Maybe she can run away," suggests Leon.

"Yeah. I want to run away, too." Kundu holds the fishing line to the kite with both hands.

"To where?" asked Lorraine.

"Ocho Rios or Montego Bay." Kundu looks back at her.

"That's far."

"My mother might live there," added Kundu.

Leon stands up, next to Kundu. "You have to take a country bus."

Kundu unwraps the wire from his hand and wraps it onto Leon's, who shimmies his hand and the kite shakes and pecks frantically. Leon releases more of the wire and the kite floats backward then dives under a gust of wind. Kites anchored to other children standing on nearby piles swoop in and out of the shadow of white clouds. More than a dozen kites, some purple, orange, blue, black and red, lunge and float in a pretty earth-blue sky freckled with cotton clouds.

A boisterous release of jumbled sounds erupts from the scattered huddles listening to the transistor radios. The West Indies had managed to take the wicket of Imran Khan, after he scored only a half century. Shouts of 'yeah!' and 'go deh!' emanated from corners, lanes, in-between zinc fences and cinder block rooms. Small children shriek as they dodged paper-stuffed milk boxes while playing Dandy Shandy.

Kundu watched his kite fly freely, climbing higher into the sky like the Cessna at Tinson Pen. His white eyelashes closed around his squinting purple eyes as he looked up at his kite as it danced high among the others. He wondered if he could build a big one, a kite big enough that he could just hold on to it and fly.

Chapter 33

Epifanie

Madda Tee and her two children squeezed begrudgingly into the single window brick room. Moses was long enough to touch three walls when he stretched his arms and legs at the same time. There was no furniture except for the plywood leaning up against the wall. The room was the same size as the outhouse built by Big Leaf in Dry Hill. It was the summer of 1969.

When Madda Tee, Moses and Epifanie arrived in Kingston, they walked along the muddy truck tire tracks to find the brick room left behind by her sister. Gurty left one month earlier as a stowaway onboard a cargo ship destined for Florida. She saved money from selling liquor in a backstreet dance hall called Tubby's.

Gurty would tell a man how strong she thought he was. She loved to feel on their biceps. She had light brown skin with freckles spattered across her face like stars across the night sky. She giggled and laughed at every word. Men from the railroad and shipping yards concentrated on the zipper of her mini skirt that seems to be on the verge of coming loose. Soon, she knew everyone's name, what they liked to drink, where they liked a rub down or a shoulder rub. Gurty was everybody's favorite. She met a ship captain at Tubby's and found her way onboard to cross the Atlantic. She folded herself into a barrel and was sent onboard in a container. As the ship eased its way out to sea, her captain friend concealed her in his room for safe keeping.

Before leaving, Gurty sent a telegram saying her brick and zinc house in Riverton City was in the third yard from Standpipe. It would be a temporary place until Madda Tee found a factory job or something. While she waited for the factory to put out a notice for seamstresses, Madda Tee found and captured a spot next to a half-coolie woman at Coronation Market. Madda Tee sold yam, okra, dasheen, pumpkin, cassava and sweet potato. She worked every day except Sunday. On Sundays she would get dressed in all white. She would read passages from her Bible aloud, while sitting on her wood and brick steps.

It was November when Epifanie's belly began to push through her main buttoned-down dress. She ignored cramps and belly aches every day, but today she couldn't stop the tears. Her arms and legs had gained size, and her once-petite frame mirrored her mother's stature in full form. Epifanie couldn't explain why she couldn't fit her one good pair of white pants she brought with her from Dry Hill. She didn't have her period for all seven months living in Riverton City. She didn't tell Moses, even though he could feel her period cramps in his belly, when they were thirteen years old. Moses didn't like Coronation Market. He said women should sell, he will hustle and run things.

After Madda Tee hit her across her back, arms and legs with a strap, Epifanie cried and vomited the six steamed okra she had eaten. Madda Tee asked her over and over, "Who you breeding fa?" She would wail down on Epifanie with every stroke. Epifanie rolled into a ball, covering her head and shoulders. The strap whistled in the air then cracked on her skin, leaving curved lines like connecting rivers of thin blood. A small crowd stood outside the yard as Epifanie's screams flared through the single window and closed door.

As if feeling the stroke of the strap, Moses pushes the door open and grabs the strap from Madda Tee, and stands between her and Epifanie.

"Lawd a Mercy, Jesus Christ. A you? You breed you sista," cried Madda Tee.

Epifanie's sobbing turned into a deep heavy groan. Madda Tee turns to Epifanie and ambles down on one knee, and then the other. She picks up the end of Epifanie's dress.

"Run go call Sista Daphne," yells Madda Tee.

Moses ran out of the single room and through a curious crowd that gathered, mumbling and pointing among themselves.

"How long it a pain you?" asked Madda Tee.

"Since last night." Epifanie catches her breath, then breathes in and out deeply and quickly, as if putting out a fire. Madda Tee covers the single box spring bed with four cardboard box containers that had a picture of a Polar fan. The box had white letters that said, 'Keep Cool.'

Madda Tee eases Epifanie away from the corner she was trapped in while getting the beating.

Epifanie rolls onto the box spring and crushed boxes, groaning loudly, holding her stomach.

Riverton City is dark at night. There are no electric poles or wires. The only light comes from kerosene lamps and outdoor pit fires. Madda Tee turns up the wick of her kerosene lamp and lights it with a short match. The light flickers through the room, casting a dark shadow of Madda Tee against the cinder block wall. Epifanie twisted and turned as her legs seemingly tried to walk away, unbeknownst to her. Sweat ran down her forehead and face, around her neck and down her back. The box beneath her was soaked through to the springs.

Epifanie cried and groaned for two more hours before Moses returned with Sista Daphne. Epifanie rocked from side to side clutching her belly and gritting her teeth. Sista Daphne opens her crocus bag and takes out a flask of white rum, a bottle of castor oil, a ratchet knife and a Bible.

"This baby coming quick," says Sista Daphne. "Go to Standpipe and get some water," she says to Moses. Moses grabs the orange plastic bucket from the side of the room and pushes his way through the door. Sista Daphne has dark skin with bone-white teeth; the right side of her forehead has a white patch of skin shaped like a flower. She has serious eyes and pointed lips.

"Pifanie...Pifanie, listen to me! You have to roll over on you knees. You hands and knees on the mattress spring," instructs Sista Daphne.

Madda Tee and Sista Daphne roll Epifanie to her side and then onto her hands and knees. Epifanie starts to slip her hands through her dress leaving her back bare and her bottom exposed.

"You have to push it out like you a doo doo. Don't worry yourself. Mi feel Jesus in this room."

Madda Tee has her eyes closed and both palms facing up as she looks towards the roof of the room. Her mouth is moving but there are no words. Moses runs into the room, his face is covered in sweat and his feet are covered in mud.

"Just leave the water at the door. You can't do nothing for her right now. Go sit down outside," ordered Sista Daphne. Moses closes the door behind him and walks to the fence of the yard. It is pitch black except for a pit fire not too far away. Moses stayed there, listening and waiting as Epifanie cried out over and over, each cry a little bit louder than the one before.

Inside of the single room now smelled of feces, vomit, kerosene and old wet clothes.

"Come on Epifanie, you have to push this baby out. Act like you a go a toilet."

Madda Tee rubs Epifanie's back then uses the sleeve from her dress to wipe her forehead.

Epifanie digs her fingers into the box spring, breaking the thin rotted cotton fabric that covers it. She rocks back and forth, stopping only to push.

"See it deh! Head a come out. Praise Jesus. Push Epifanie," encourages Sista Daphne.

"*Real real real,*" sings Madda Tee.

"*Christ so real to me.*

I love him because he give us the victory.

Many people doubt him,

but I can't live without him,

that is why I love him so,

he so real to me."

She takes a tambourine from her plastic bucket and sings the same song again loudly.

Epifanie is breathing heavier, then wails at the top of her lungs. Each cycle of sound ravages the still darkness that surrounds Riverton City.

"See the head yah. The baby a come. Push it out. Push it! Yes gyaal! Push it out," yells Sista Daphne. Epifanie holds on to the cinder block under the box spring and digs her nails into it as far as they could bend.

Madda Tee is singing again.

"*What a friend we have in Jesus*

He's as bright as morning start

He's the fairest of ten thousand
Everybody ought to know
Everybody ought to know
Everybody ought to know
Who Jesus is."

Epifanie roars as the baby comes rolling into the arms of Sista Daphne. He's wet and slippery, like a yellow eel. His mouth opens with a soft cry at first, then shifts into a full alarm. His hair is white. His body glowed from the kerosene lamp's steady light.

Madda Tee gives Sista Daphne a white cotton skirt with smattered old stains. Sista Daphne puts the baby down on the skirt. Epifanie rolls over onto her back and looks at her baby. Sista Daphne pours white rum in a plastic jar then submerges the ratchet knife's blade. The cardboard on top of the box spring is soaked through with water from Epifanie. Sista Daphne ties a knot in the umbilical cord. She takes the knife from the jar of rum and cuts the cord. Epifanie stares at her baby, as tears and sweat roll down her face. Her knuckles were bleeding, and she could taste splinters of teeth in her mouth.

Madda Tee's mouth is once again moving without words.

"No wonder this baby so stubborn. A boy you have. Him skin yellow like you or even white," says Sista Daphne as she wraps the baby in the white skirt. She gives the baby to Madda Tee, who continues to pray silently. Madda Tee hands her new grandson to his mother, who holds the baby close to her chest against her naked body. The baby's eyelashes are long and white, like his hair. He opens his eyes slowly, they are dark, but she could see herself reflected in them. He closed his eyes again. She could feel his heart thumping little soft thumps, quickly, like a frightened little bird sitting in the hand of a stranger.

"We have to take out the afterbirth," says Sista Daphne. She looks at Epifanie's face. "What him name?"

"Kundu," smiles Epifanie.

"Kundu?" replies Sista Daphne.

"That's Big Leaf's name." Madda Tee turns her head and wipes her face and forehead.

"My grandfather is Kundu. Dem call him Big Leaf, but his real name was Kundu."

Madda Tee covers her face and cries into her hands. "Mi sorry baby. Mi sorry. Mi no want you fi end up like me. Look where we are. You think say a this mi want for you? And now you have baby. Lawd God, it hard. It hard bad. Mi sorry, mi sorry. Oh God, Lawd have mercy pon we."

Moses comes into the room and stands at the door. Epifanie looks up at him and then down at Kundu.

"Leave this yard. No come back here," screamed Madda Tee. "A you a Satan. Go way!"

Moses walks backward while looking at Epifanie and Kundu. Sista Daphne is wrapping the afterbirth in a plastic bag. Epifanie wipes her tears off Kundu's face and holds him close to her chest.

If We Must Die

The lanes and dirt roads are usually quiet when the sun sits directly above. Stray dogs with protruding ribs and spines languish in the shade. They are two or three generations of mongrels, void of any identifiable clues that would give away their breed. They were just...dogs.

Although the sky was clear and the sun was a ball sent from hell, there was news of a hurricane coming to the island, on its way from the Lesser Antilles. The news carried by the market women says that it killed one hundred people already. Storms and hurricanes are normal in Jamaica. Everyone would add extra nails or zinc to keep their house or shed intact. Police would advise everyone to stay away from the street and hide in their homes, preferably under their beds. The news says the hurricane was called Allan.

Allan was out at sea and was making its way up the coast slowly, but with strong winds that reached up to one hundred and ninety miles per hour. The Joncrow birds remain committed to the sky, as they search majestically above the rotting piles for food. They are usually invisible during the rains and heavy storms. Today they lorded above the heap and over the dry dirt and gravel. With sharp eyes, they can pick off a mouse from a condensed milk can trapped under rotted wooden doors.

Kundu, Lorraine and Leon walk in single file through a narrow dogless lane, each carrying a plastic bucket of water.

"Mi tired," Leon begins to whine. He puts the bucket down, then sits down. Kundu takes his bucket off his head and lays it on the uneven gravel and sand. Lorraine lays hers next to Kundu.

"You think is Blackheart Man kill Peta-Gay like them say?" asked Lorraine.

"Must be blackheart man do things like that. Makka Beard say a wicked people and parasite mek them things happen." Kundu skips away from a blue ground lizard.

"Parasite? Parasite like worm?" asked Leon.

"Like worm in you belly. Them live off you food and suck you blood," Kundu warns.

"Somebody drag her off into a car. She not going with no man," states Lorraine. "She probably walking in the lane and somebody jump out and drag her inside."

"Maybe a shotta." Leon kicks a bottle cap far ahead of them.

"If somebody come near me, I'm stabbing them." Lorraine takes a two-inch brown handle flip knife from her waist. "Maybe the shotta or even Junjo the Don Man."

Kundu looks at the knife. "Where you find that?"

"It was my mother." She pulls the brown rusted blade from the handle and stares at it.

"Can I touch it?" asked Leon. Lorraine looks at Leon with raised eyebrows.

"Just a little bit." Lorraine closed the knife and handed it to him. Leon holds it to the sky as if to inspect it for imperfections.

"Nobody dragging me in them car. They have to kill me. My sister tell me that." Lorraine nods her head.

"What if is more than one of them? You have to run." says Kundu.

"And you a girl, man faster than you." Leon interjects.

"Mi faster than you," replied Lorraine.

"Lie! A big lie that. You ever beat me yet?"

"A true, she run leave you the other day," Kundu pointed out.

"Mi foot was hurting me. Let's race right now," dares Leon.

Kundu smiles a little. "Race with the bucket on your head."

"Alright." Lorraine puts her bucket on her head between her two pigtails. Kundu levels the bucket on his uneven bone-white hair. He straightens his neck without spilling the water.

Leon squats as he picks up the bucket and levels it on his low-cut hair. His hair was cut in school after the school nurse found lice and ringworm on his head.

"On your mark, get set, go!" yelled Leon.

Lorraine and Leon rub shoulders and elbows, bumping buckets and spilling splashes of water. Kundu races behind them as Leon jolts his way to the front.

"Whoever is last, a Junkanoo," shouts Leon. They race through the lane, guided by shoulder-high fences. Leon comes out of the lane first and sets his bucket down next to Aunt Pet's front step.

"Afternoon, Ms. Aunt Pet," stumbles Leon. Lorraine, followed by Kundu, come out of the lane and set their buckets next to Leon's.

"Afternoon, Ms. Aunt Pet." Kundu sits next to Leon.

"Aunt Pet, we get some bathing water," announces Lorraine.

A stout Joncrow bird ruffles its black wings high at the top of the heap facing Aunt Pet's unpainted single room zinc, wood and brick house. The bird stared, its jet-black eyes looking into Aunt Pet's.

Lorraine takes her bucket inside. Kundu picks up his bucket and places it at the door. Leon gives Kundu his bucket and he places it at the door once more. Lorraine takes the buckets. Aunt Pet sits still in her chair, her unblinking eyes are grey with little streams of tears that were almost dried against her jowl cheeks. Her chest was still, it neither inflated nor deflated, as most great-chested women do. She was quiet and motionless as the bird, as if locked in a child's game of who blinks first.

Lorraine comes out of the room with a copper mug of water. "I'm going to boil some cornmeal porridge." She walks over to the fire pit and places the copper mug on rocks.

"Lorraine," says Kundu softly. "Come see."

Lorraine walks onto the small plywood stoop. Aunt Pet's head of hair was reduced to patches of greying stubbles, not unlike scrubbing tools used on large black pots for outdoor cooking. Lorraine touches Aunt Pet's elbow, then gets closer, pressing her ear on Aunt Pet's chest.

"She not breathing." Lorraine is frightened.

"She dead?" asked Leon.

"Run go Standpipe and tell the police them," says Kundu to Leon.

Leon straightens the back of his shoes and covers his heels. He sprints to the narrow lane and pumps his arms while running. Lorraine and Kundu stood next to Aunt Pet, as she stared at the clear sky that would slowly develop into a sunset. Her view changed when the first of the new plastic dumps were ordered by the Sanitation Department. She could still see the sunset, but under the shadow of a dried stinking mountain of white and clear plastic containers.

Kundu and Lorraine watched as four more Joncrow birds assembled. They gathered and formed an audience of eager onlookers. Their dark suits, modest and respectful of the dead, glistened like angels of the sun, witnesses to a last rite. Lorraine looked back through the open door of the little house. She could see the springless mat on which she and Aunt Pet slept. It smelled of moth balls and Vicks Vapor rub, where Lorraine would bathe, clean and feed Aunt Pet. It had been Lorraine's job since she was ten years old.

Kundu stood next to Aunt Pet and Lorraine as they all stared back at the birds, locked in the child's game: whosoever blinked first was out.

Chapter 35

Standpipe

I t's Tuesday August 5th at 6pm. The MP, Mr. George Douglas, calls for an impromptu meeting at Standpipe. His pickup truck, plastered with red stickers and bright red and orange markers, was parked in front of the clean water pipe where everyone walked to collect water with bucket or barrel. He was flanked by four blue-uniformed policemen, with six more adorned with black, short nozzle machine guns slung across their torsos, standing around the perimeter. Their helmets and boots matched the guns they carried. They all seemed tall and sleek, like they could run the 100-meter, like Olympic champion Don Quarrie.

Both Radio Jamaica and Jamaica Broadcasting Station reported that Hurricane Allan was only two days away from Jamaica. The winds were less violent and were recorded at a maximum of one hundred and fifty-four miles per hour. Hurricane Allan was the biggest hurricane on record. Mr. Douglas stands in the back of his pickup truck with a white and red megaphone to his lips.

"Comrades! Comrades! We have two months before election. I see a lot of green on fences and walls. Like the Laborite them trying to take over Riverton City. A fi we ground this! This a PNP power. I will tell you this, that if I go to sleep and dreams say I turn Laborite, I won't bother to wake up. I would rather die in my sleep. We not going to give Riverton to them wokliss boy. What him name? Trinity. Them have them badman, we have our badman them too. Them have gun, but we have our things them too. Two things we come to tell you. We know everybody a fret about the missing girls. We find all six of them, but regrettably it was too late. We pledge to you on this day, that we will find the criminal or criminals responsible and punish with the full force of the penal code. Whoever did this deserves to die. And I wouldn't be shocked if this animal was a Laborite."

The MP swipes his forehead with a cloth and continues.

"The next thing I want to tell you about is this Hurricane Allan. If you have somewhere you can cotch or stay for a few days, I would go now! This hurricane is no piah piah hurricane. It lick down Haiti and Dominica, mash up Puerto Rico and coming this way. This thing is going to be wicked. Don't think say because nothing happened to you during the last storm everything alright. Puss and dog no have the same luck. This is not a storm; this is a Category Five hurricane. I will tell you again, those who can leave, leave. If you can't leave, get some extra nail and wood to make your place stronger. The Peoples National Party will send extra plywood for those who want it."

He steps down from the truck as murmurs rise among the confused faces.

"How we go get the wood?" A voice emerges from the murmur. MP Douglas waves his hand and gets into the passenger side of his pickup truck. Junjo appears from behind and is standing on the edge of an incidental circle formed by trucks passing around the elevated standpipe water shed.

Junjo stands next to the truck by the passenger window.

"Constable tell you right?" asked MP Douglas.

"'Bout what?" Junjo leans into the door.

"The man that you kill the other day."

"A which man me kill? Nobody never see me kill anyone."

"Look! Whether is you kill him or not, his brother is making up a whole lotta noise how him going to burn this place to the ground. How him going to kill everybody, from old man to pickney."

"Make him come! We not running." Junjo adjusts the small gun stuck in his waist. "That's why we ask for the Chopper them. We want the same thing that the police have."

"You have to wait until after this hurricane thing is over. As soon as it pass, come check me." The MP's truck pulls away through the crowd.

"Alright, easy." says Junjo. He walks back into the milling crowd and murmurs, followed by shottas. They were camouflaged among and within the chattering stressed faces. Baby Face Shotta fires six shots in the air, followed by the other shottas in response. A circle of smoke travels up above them. They walk slowly down the main dirt road, clinging to the sides, brushing the fences with their hands and guns. They follow Junjo into a lane. Hungry stray dogs follow behind the last lanky shotta, as he strolls leisurely like a giraffe on the high plains.

The wind is stronger than it was an hour ago. Suddenly, the bleak greyish light behind the clouds was wiped away, and darkness at 8pm fell like sudden midnight. Faces at the standpipe moved through the maze of narrow lanes. Loose sheets of zinc panels clank and scrape among themselves. The mongrel dogs, sniffing and bobbing their heads, skip away from the headless feet and legs stampeding through darkened lanes and narrow creases. Winds rushing through the cone shaped dump piles in the distance, blanket the air with sour fruit, burnt wood and something dead or rusty.

Chapter 36

The Dundus

Epifanie saved all the money she made selling roast corn on the edge of Coronation Market. She stuffed her dirty beige drawstring bag with the white jeans she negotiated down from four dollars to two. Her soap, deodorant and hairbrush were already tucked into the bottom, along with a blouse and underwear. The light from Madda Tee's kerosene lamp flickered, then settled into a steady burn. There is a rusted pot covered with cardboard in the corner of the room. Next to it is a hand-sized plastic bottle with a nipple cover.

Kundu is sleeping in a frayed bamboo basket on the opposite side. His nappy is held together by giant blue dolphin pins that stick out at the side. Epifanie crawls on her hands and knees across Madda Tee's bed, then onto her cardboard cot next to Kundu. Six mosquitoes had landed on his belly, arms, legs and forehead. Epifanie waved her hand and they all scatter. She scurried around the room on her knees until she killed them all. Kundu opens his eyes, and she picks him up and cradles him in her arms, then pulls her tank top up and Kundu latches on to her. His eyes, looking up at her, are dark and colorless in the light. Kundu's white little fingers pats her nose and flutters around her angled face. Epifanie moves her fingers through his hair and he smiles with shallow dimples. She pulls his nappy up towards his protruding navel, then runs her fingers across his white eyebrows and pulls on his earlobe. Kundu smiles, exposing his gums, then latches on to Epifanie again; his eyes are fixed onto hers.

Epifanie looks to the slightly opened plywood door. The roaring engine of a late dump truck causes the room to vibrate and chatter.

Epifanie sings quietly,

"If you miss the train I'm on,

then you know that I am gone.

And you can hear the whistle blow a hundred miles.

A hundred miles, a hundred miles, a hundred miles, a hundred miles

You can hear the whistle blow

A hundred miles."

Kundu kicks his legs as if he's riding a bicycle and smiles up at his mother.

The dull thud of footsteps brushing against the plywood ramp leading to the door breaks the quietness of the room. Madda Tee steps into the room and plops down a red and orange crocus bag in the corner away from Epifanie and Kundu. She bends down on one knee and then eases onto her box spring bed. "Lawd have his mercy. I tired."

Epifanie looks down and rocks Kundu.

"A where you going tonight?" asked Madda Tee.

Epifanie looks up at her. Madda Tee takes off her light blue plastic slippers and puts them against the grey concrete wall.

"I have a job interview." says Epifanie.

"With who?"

"Darlene say she know a man that need people to work at the resort."

"At night? What typa job that?

Epifanie rubs Kundu's soft hair while looking in his eyes. "Dance for tourist."

Madda Tee sits with her back against the wall. "Oh Lawd. Dance where?"

"It pay nuff money."

"Nuff money. Where?" Madda Tee asked again.

"Ocho Rios. I can work, save up some money and buy a house. I can send for you and…"

"Send for who? You taking the baby with you."

"No." says Epifanie. She pulls her tank top down and holds up Kundu, then eases him into basket. He sticks out his legs and rolls down back to the cardboard. "I'm coming back for him."

Kundu stands up wobbling back and forth and side to side. He takes a step, then settles himself with his arms high. He takes two more steps and holds on to Epifanie.

"Is because the people them a talk?" asked Madda Tee. "Is not them business. Dem a call him duppy and ghost. Dem stupid! Nothing no wrong with him, nothing."

"That's why I have to go," insists Epifanie. "We can't live here. We neva come a Kingston to live in a dump ground."

"So, you just all of a sudden leaving now. Tonight? Lawd have mercy."

Epifanie stands up then kneels before Kundu. She pulls him close to her chest and prays.

"The light of God surrounds you.

The love of God enfolds you.

The power of God protects you.

The presence of God watches over you.

Wherever you are, God is, my son."

She puts Kundu next to Madda Tee as he stuffs four of his fingers into his mouth. Epifanie picks up her drawstring bag and opens the door. She looks back at Madda Tee, who looks away towards Kundu. Epifanie steps through the door and down the plywood ramp. She runs through the open gates of the yard, then stops and hunches over as her head and body convulses while clutching her stomach. She wipes her mouth with her hand cloth then starts running again.

Madda Tee stands at the door with Kundu in her arms.

Epifanie fades into the darkness.

Chapter 37

Aunt Pet

Aunt Pet's plywood casket sits atop four bricks in front of the pulpit. The ruffle of paper fans seems to chatter in clicks and sighs. The fanning spreads the sour smell of underarm sweat masked with flower-scented deodorant. The doors of the church are open wide along with the windows. Pastor Beloved wipes his sweat with the end of the white towel draped over his shoulder. Men with broad shoulders turn slightly in or out to fit between the uneven pews.

Aunt Pet lived in Riverton City before the church was built. She prayed for Pastor Beloved. She prayed over newborn babies, she prayed over storms and even cricket wins for the West Indies team. Aunt Pet prayed in patois and then in tongues. She would cry and sob so Jesus would notice her and answer her crying.

If a child had a fever, Aunt Pet would get a knock on her door. She would walk in the dark whispering scriptures as she made her way to the sick. She was the prayer lady, and no one bothered her. The news of prayers that were answered on the good side spread through Riverton City and cast a shadow over all the other prayers that were not so fortunate. When Aunt Pet's sister died, she took charge of eight-year-old Lorraine and her fourteen-year-old sister Millicent. There were five people living in the windowless room. It was patched together by rope, nails, cement, and plywood.

On Easter Sunday, the police came to the church after she fainted in the choir seats. The choir was in the first verse of *Praise My Soul the King of Heaven*. They said she had a stroke because of the blood pressure or the heat. Aunt Pet never sang or spoke again. When Ms. Gogo came to collect Millicent, Pet tried to speak with all her might but no words came. Ms. Gogo told Aunt Pet that her sister Marva owed her a lot of money. Now she's dead, how's she going to get her money back? She did, however, believe that Millicent would be better off if she would come and live with her and work off the debt. Plus, she would have a roof over her head and still go to school. Aunt Pet stared without moving.

Millicent rolled her church dress into a ball along with her shorts and blue jeans. She stuffed them into a paper bag, and forced her feet into her flat shoes, one foot brown and the other black. Lorraine stood in the corner of the room and watched Millicent walk out with Ms. Gogo, passing Aunt Pet in her chair. As Ms. Gogo drove off with a police car in front and behind her car, a thick ball of tears rolled down Aunt Pet's face into her twisted half-opened mouth. Lorraine ran behind the car as it slowly eased its way through the lane. Aunt Pet was fixed in her chair. Silent.

Lorraine chased Ms. Gogo's car until it made a left turn at Standpipe, then sped off onto the highway.

The hair bun Millicent fixed for her was now flopped open and hung around her face and neck like the tears streaking from her eyes. Millicent was gone, too.

Chapter 38

Two Days to Allan

Two dump trucks rumbled through the lane; the second truck tightly tucked behind the tail of the other. The drivers changed gears and revved the engines to explode dark thick smoke. The wheels of the trucks spit mud and dog shit on the side of the rust and silver zinc fences. Small children race behind the truck followed by their parents and able-bodied adults, to the dump pile where parts of furniture and big garbage are piled. A drizzle of hot rain falls like tears from the greying black clouds that resemble mountains in the sky.

The trucks disappear through the lanes, but their belching and cough-like sounds still ring through the narrow fences. Men and boys, some shirtless, hammer nails into fences and plywood. Some were busy draping tarpaulins over open spaces between the concrete walls and the roof. A breeze fights through the twist and turns of the lanes and whistles through holes of nailed down zinc fences. The cricket men with the transistor radio say that Hurricane Allan would land in Ocho Rios, then Port Maria and down into Port Antonio first, then move through to Kingston. Radio Jamaica says the winds are sustained at one hundred and seventy miles an hour.

MP Clive Barrett sent a pick-up truck with ten pieces of yellow plywood for anyone who needs an extra door. He told the waiting crowd of about two hundred men and women that the shortage was due to the JLP Laborite greed, and that they should remember to vote for the Peoples National Party. MP Barrett flipped a smile exposing his one gold tooth next to his chalk-white originals.

The little light from the sun, disallowed by the stubborn darkness of the cloud, is losing the battle. The devil and his wife are no longer fighting. The sun had officially lost and darkness had settled in like a lazy cow, too heavy to be moved and didn't answer to prayers or foul language. Rumbling thunder dropped from heaven after lightning cracked through the darkness and filled the sky. It was nighttime, but the five o'clock news peppered with static surges, rose through and around the narrow walkways from radios held preciously by old men. A hundred people had perished in the Dominican Republic on account of Allan. The hurricane winds were battering Port Antonio, even though Allan hadn't gotten there yet, the radio said. A flash of lightning streaks across Riverton City, sparking against an old water pipe someone had used to erect a cross. It sparked and spewed smoke. At the base of the dump pile, a bony dog lays lifeless among a bike motor, broken bar stool and cracked bauxite bricks. His bones were sticking out of his ribs and his mouth stayed open with tongue hanging out to the side of his jaw. There was a hole in the top of his forehead filled with maggots. There were no Joncrow birds in the sky. The dog laid unmolested, except for a circus buzzing of thick black flies, diving in and out with an angry chorus of fly songs.

"Watch out for the mawga dog," says Leon.

Lorraine kissed her teeth. "Dog dead. Him not biting you."

"Mi no care. Not walking over him." Leon skips to the other side.

Kundu teases Leon. "You think him might turn into duppy and bite you."

"Duppy dog? Dog can turn into duppy?" asked Leon, puzzled.

Kundu crosses the street and Lorraine and Leon follow, each carrying empty aluminum oil pans converted to water containers. As they approach Standpipe, a congregation of people bustled around the water stand, taking turns to fill their buckets, bottles, calabash, and bedpans. People were walking hurriedly into the mud circle. It was the only clean watering area, and a gateway for trucks to enter with their giant wheels and smoky pipe. As Kundu approaches the water stand, the chatter becomes lower. He fills his oil pan. Leon and Lorraine move rapidly as the annoyed voices seem to rise again. There is a rush of raindrops popping on zinc.

Like horses lining up for a race, bare feet, basket-weaved slippers, and old shoes splash through the mud and sink holes left by giant tires. Kundu, Lorraine and Leon are running with their pans of water on their heads.

Leon starts the chant. "Rain a fall breeze a blow, chicken batty outta door."

"Rain a fall breeze a blow, chicken batty outta door," repeat Kundu and Lorraine.

They ran down the lane, weaving through the anxious mob of wet faces, arms and legs that carried water of their own. Pieces of loose zinc clank and chattered as it railed against wobbling fences. Loose boxes, paper plates, newspaper and condensed milk cans rushed down the lane, then swirled in a circle. They suddenly disappear into the air then fall from the darkened sky. More cans and paper fly into the circle, then disappear. Fresh green paint spelling 'JLP' splattered the unpainted walls of the houses and zinc fence of the main truck lane. There was a man pitched forward on his face with both arms by his side. There was a brush and open can of paint on its side next to him. The hurried crowd had slowed down then stopped. The children stood behind them, looking between arms and torsos, legs and shoulders.

A voice announced, "Him dead!" More murmurs swell.

"Dem shot him?" asked another voice.

"It looks like dem stab him," replied the first voice.

"How much stab him get?"

"I don't know. But him definitely dead."

"Must be the Trinity man from Rema."

"I hear say him no use gun. Him like fi look into you face when you a dead."

"Trinity? Him a Father, Son and Holy Ghost. A blasphemy that. Like him a god."

"A one a Junjo boy them this. Him a shotta."

A man with a lantern walks over to the body. The shotta was face down into a circle of his own blood. His knitted undershirt was torn and ripped where his belly was punctured. Thick blood clustered around his neck and around his mouth. The stray pack of mongrel dogs waiting on the side, happily dip their tongues into bloodied water rushing through the muddy creases next to the fence. Madda Tee's fence had fresh green paint that said JLP too, but the 'J" was crossed out and a 'P' was halfway complete. The paint stroke dragged to the bottom of the fence and into the dirt and blood.

Leon ducks between the wet stale stench of people, trying to remember the name of the young boy. He was face down in the red and black mud peppered with open cans, broken bottles and pages from the newspaper. Lorraine and Kundu follow closely behind Leon. Kundu walks closely against the fence, looking down with his water bucket on his head. He steps on something hard in the mud. His big toe had dug into something with a hole. Kundu stops and rests his water bucket against the fence and picked up his foot.

"What is that?" asked Lorraine.

"Blouse nawt! Hide it." Leon is startled.

"A gun. Put it back." urges Lorraine. Kundu puts his foot back in the mud.

"Hide it." Leon whispered softly.

Kundu bends down and picks up the gun and forces it into his pants pocket.

"Maybe we can hide it," says Kundu.

"Where?" Lorraine is puzzled.

"I don't want a gun. Karate people don't need gun," Leon shrugs.

Lorraine suddenly stops. "Maybe a this shotta kill Peta-Gaye."

"Or maybe rolling calf." Leon interrupts.

"Everything is rolling calf." Lorraine scoffs.

"The gun is probably the shotta own," says Kundu as he adjusts his pants waist.

Kundu and Leon go into the yard. Madda Tee's usual fire pit was dark. The ashes were spread throughout the yard resting in small puddles. Leon's square room house was dark except for a small candle flicker coming from under the plywood door. Darlene opens the door and stands halfway in.

She is not dressed up today. Her hair is wrapped in a yellow and black handkerchief, and her dress was banana yellow. No one dared to wear red, orange, green or cyan. The right color could determine a suspicious nod. The wrong color could start a festival of bullets.

"Bring the water nuh!" Darlene shouts between the wind and bullet raindrops. Her arm was wrapped in an old cloth diaper that slung around her neck and arm.

"Later," Leon calls out, looking back at Kundu and Lorraine. He walks hurriedly towards Darlene and up the wooden platform into the square concrete house.

"All a you should go inside," shouts Darlene. She points to Madda Tee's house, and walks in behind Leon, closing the door.

"Kundu, don't turn into shotta. I feel like one of the shotta them kill Peta-Gay. If you turn shotta we not friends anymore." Lorraine shakes the rain from her face.

"Me, shotta? I'm going to hide it so no other shotta can find it and kill somebody."

A gust of wind dives in and around them, whipping rain horizontally against their faces. The popping sounds of heavy raindrops on zinc gets louder.

"Did you ask her?" Lorraine puts the water bucket by the outhouse walls.

"No, I'm going ask now." He walks up the plywood ramp. Madda Tee's kerosene lamp flickers under the door. Lorraine stands behind Kundu in the doorway.

"What you leave the door open for?" Madda Tee sits up slowly.

Kundu takes another step forward and Lorraine appears from behind him, and closes the door.

"Oh!" says Madda Tee. "Sorry for your Aunt Pet. Couldn't come to the funeral. Foot a hurt me." She sits up on her box spring bed and adjusts her brassiere. The wind howls then whistle through the one-inch space between the roof and the concrete walls.

"She don't have anybody over there. She can stay here until the storm gone?" blurts out Kundu.

Lorraine looks away from Madda Tee's grey-eyed stare. Madda Tee pushes herself forward and grunts while standing up halfway. She rocks backward and plops back onto the box spring. Her shadow on the wall is twice her size.

"Knock on Ms. V door. Tell her I want to talk to her."

Kundu walks out and knocks on Ms. V's plywood door. Ms. V comes out covered in a black plastic tablecloth with a hole cut out of the middle, revealing her head.

Ms. V and Madda Tee talked in big people whispers, then Ms V. told Lorraine to get her clothes and come back to her house before the hurricane gets worst. Lorraine can stay with her.

Chapter 39

Beverly Hills

The alarm clock with two silver bells on top like bunny ears, says it's 4:30AM. Millicent pulls the sheet over her head. Butch stands in the corner of her small room, stretching his marina over his ruffled head of hair. He opens the door and saunters through while glancing back at her. As he closes the door, Millicent jumps from the single bed and grabs her flower yellow nightie. She steps through and pulls it over her thin shaking body. Beverly Hills at night is always quiet. Except for the high-pitched motor buzzing of lawn mowers, the days were quiet too.

Hurricane Allan did not care. Winds and sideways rain crashed into the rich houses on the hill and pummeled roofs and windows with indiscriminate anger. The radio reported that Allan did not arrive yet. Glass windows that functioned only for the rich to leer out at ordinary people and their ordinary lives, were battened down with four-by-four wood and steel grills.

Butch's late-night visits to Millicent's little room in the back of the house are always followed by tears. Ms. Gogo bought him a red Volkswagen Bug one month ago for his birthday. She asked Millicent if she thought he was strapping. Millicent didn't look at her but continued to mop the tile floor. Millicent mopped the floors every day. Ms. Gogo showed her how to make Chow Fun, Chop Suey and her favorite Jamaican Chinese dishes.

Ms. Gogo's husband went back to China for business. He was gone for two months now and had not called.

Every house in Beverly Hills Jamaica had a helper living in a little room in the back corner of the house. When the Misses of the house went shopping or left to inspect the family business, the helpers would find an area close to the property edges and work alongside the helper next door.

The whispers now said Mr. Gogo was actually never coming back. He was at least seventy. Ms. Gogo's family gave their blessing to the marriage. She was eighteen when she quietly said 'I Do' in front of two hundred cousins and friends in Hong Kong.

Now Ms. Gogo is thirty-eight, with strong thighs and back, flowing black hair and pointed red lips. Mr. Gogo walks behind her with his cane, coughing and spitting up his grey and green consumption. The extra fat from his belly stretches over his ribs then across his humped back. They own a store in the Uptown Shopping Plaza. It sold toy airplanes, tricycles, jeans, fluffy dresses and Clarkes Booties.

Ms. Gogo would give Millicent a blouse or dress that had a stubborn zipper or the loose stitching on the wrong side. Millicent would take it with a smile while holding it up against her shoulders. Her mother Marva taught her to look the opposite of what she feels. 'If you feel bad, no mek nobody know, smile and go about you business.' Millicent could hear her mother's voice as if she was sitting next to her. Millicent kept herself neat. Even the baggiest pass-down from Ms. Gogo was pinned and buttoned without notice. She learned how to sew by hand and needle from her mother.

Millicent kept Ms. Gogo's house neat, too. The house is perched on the windward side of Beverly Hills overlooking the densely lit Kingston. The pillows, the sheets, the books, the pots, and the plates were all arranged by size or sometimes color. She separated Ms. Gogo's pills and medications by day or night usage: day pills and medications were on the bottom shelf, and night pills and everything else were kept on the top shelf. Millicent once counted twenty-eight bottles in the cabinet. Most of them have a skull and an X. The yellow warning said to take only at night.

All the bottles were labeled for Ms. Gogo Ma.

The wind is howling lowly like a train far away but steadily approaching. Millicent sits on the floor in her little room. The winds scream across the roof and shakes the French windows, causing a loud rattle. If the roof comes tumbling down, it's best to be on the floor, her father George used to say. She couldn't remember his face, or at least most of it.

He was going to send for her, too, when he got to the States. He called her Mumpsy.

They would sit by the side of the road and watch the cars race by. He loved cars, so Millicent loved cars too. She would yell out, Escort, Jaguar, BMW, VW Bug and Capri. She would pretend that she was driving with her father George as she sat next to him. They would sit by the roadside for hours.

As she sits waiting for Hurricane Allan to come, she tries harder to remember his face. She shuts her eyes, squeezing them tightly and fights to remember. Slowly, she sees his face as it was by the docks, on the night he left for America.

"I soon come, Mumpsy," said George. He walked slowly up the ramp until he reached the top. He turned and waved goodbye. His face was coming back now. She could touch his dark skin, his broad nose. She remembers the smell of his feet, how they burned through the smell of Riverton City's freshest dump. She missed them too. The house trembles and creaks as the winds hover above, then slaps the windows and barricades. She was sure she would never see him again, either.

Chapter 40

Duppy

A full sheet of zinc, recently detached from a fledgling fence, whisks by Lorraine and Kundu. They walk swiftly, ducking and weaving through the darkness and an erratic howling wind. They know where the holes, and sharp, broken bottles await. They turn through a narrow lane that can fit only one person at a time. When they raced each other, whoever was in front would always win. Tonight, they run their fingers along the fence as they scurry, hunched over, heads down, avoiding torn zinc, nails and feces. Lorraine gets out of the narrow lane first.

The path opens up in front of Aunt Pet's little house. Everything is pitch black, except for Kundu. His pale skin moved through the darkness like the moon. Lorraine could not make out the color of his eyes. He stands at attention, looking from side to side, checking behind and in front of him.

"Wait for me. I'm going to get my bag and change clothes," whispered Lorraine.

Kundu stands by the plywood ramp that leads to the front door. Lorraine walks and reaches for the lamp on the floor. She picks up a box of matches from the floor and takes out one of two that were left by Aunt Pet, lighting the wick of the kerosene lantern tucked in the corner of the room. Next to the lantern was a purple enamel wash pan, a used bar of carbolic soap, and a dark, deceptively heavy Dutch pot.

Lorraine strikes the match and lights the wick. The light blooms against the exposed cinder block walls. There are no windows. Aunt Pet always had the door slightly open when she used the kerosene lamp. Lorraine sees a lump move, then it sits up against the wall.

Baby Face Shotta is looking at Lorraine's feet and then into her eyes. Lorraine looks at the door that is slightly open. He holds up a half-empty bottle of white rum and points the head towards Lorraine.

The kerosene lamp flickers, then recovers as a minor gust of wind slides through the door.

Baby Face Shotta takes a gulp from the bottle and makes a face. He punches his chest as if to help the rum pass his heart. Lorraine is frozen on the uneven gravel floor next to two refrigerator boxes covered with crocus bags, old pants and blankets sewn together. Aunt Pet would sleep on the left side, next to the wash pan.

"You know me?" Baby Face Shotta coughs.

"Yes," said Lorraine. She looks down and then towards the door.

"Watch here. A long time I a watch you. From you small. I know say you mother."

Lorraine looks towards the door. "No, she my auntie."

"You auntie, yeah. I know she would like me. A you a church girl. You auntie gone now, so a time for a man to move in and take care a things. Me a capture this place. You understand?" He takes another gulp from the bottle. "You do it yet? You a Virgin Mary? The obeah woman say that virgin blood can cure manhood problem. Cure for the drip-drip. Just gimme a jook. Mi know say you pum pum must fresh."

Lorraine looks back at the door still swinging back and forth from the wind and rain; she stands frozen next to the wall.

He unbuckles his belt and puts the quarter bottle of rum next to his hip.

A giant breath of wind rocks through the slightly open plywood door. The newly arrived bullet rain slashes through the door and pelts the refrigerator box bed. Kundu runs into the room, soaked from head to toe. Baby Face Shotta has his pants down to his knees, but stops moving and stares at Kundu. The rain and wind get louder as one beats on the zinc roof and the other lifts it from the foundation. Kundu looks at Lorraine and then at Baby Face Shotta in the opposite corner. Kundu's eyes appear red in the light.

Thunderous bangs of flying wood, scrap metal, furniture, soda bottles and aluminum sidings crashed into each other outside. Walls, fences, and stray bolts of lightning race through the darkness. Aunt Pet's door was off the hinges and was now a part of the dirt and tar floor. George promised to get more tar to fix the floor before he went to America. He made many promises.

"Duppy is here," Baby Face Shotta laughs with a rattle in his voice. "I hear say you can chat to dead people. A true? You must be a living duppy. Only duppy can see duppy."

He picks up his bottle and takes another gulp, falling to his side, then rolling over to his knees. He has on black and white spotted boxer shorts with his jeans by his knees and a dirty white undershirt shirt. He pushes himself up onto one knee with the bottle in one hand, and the other on the floor. He stands up and leans against the cold cinder block wall. A gun falls to the floor as his pants crumbles around his ankles. Lorraine's chest is expanding and contracting visibly. Kundu reaches around his back and takes out the revolver he found next to the dead shotta.

"Take you thing." Kundu speaks without looking away from Baby Face Shotta. Lorraine takes a big crocus bag and begins to stuff clothes, a brush, a pair of black dress shoes and two books. Kundu points the revolver at Baby Face Shotta's feet. His eyes glimmered with a light tint of red. His bare feet, shins and knees were covered in dark mud. His hand trembled with the gun.

Kundu stares without blinking his eyes. Baby Face Shotta grabs his chest, then punches his chest plate. He coughs heavily, spewing spit into the wind rushing through the door.

"Oh, a you a big don now. You have gun. You turn bad man." Baby Face Shotta is doubled over with his hands on his knees.

Lorraine stands behind Kundu, and they both walk backwards through the door.

"I will see you again, ghost." Baby Face Shotta coughs and vomits into the wall.

Kundu and Lorraine run into the dark through the narrow lane, dodging and hunkering beneath flying bed sheets, plywood doors, empty barrels and rusty sheets of zinc. Kundu runs behind Lorraine, looking back at the narrow opening of the lane. Rain beats against their face as small puddles of muddy water splash under their bare feet. They turn onto the main road, where the trucks had carved out a windy path with tires almost as tall as Lorraine. They run past Jomo's dark yard. He didn't come running after them as he always did. A strong giant wind pushes Lorraine and Kundu backwards. They turned their bodies sideways and lower their heads, leaning forward and looking out for flying pieces from the garbage mountains.

They find Madda Tee's little gate wedged into the mud. Kundu and Lorraine crouch between Madda Tee's square room and Ms. V's, which had been recently splattered with lime green paint. Kundu searches his pockets, turning them inside out.

"Lost it?" mouthed Lorraine.

Kundu nods his head. They could hear Ms. V talking loudly.

"Oh God, oh everlasting Father. I pray for your mercy and your forgiveness, Father. I love you, oh Jesus. Show me some mercy, oh Father. Oh, Father God, you are mighty and worthy of praise, oh God."

Hurricane Allan had settled next to Jamaica, said the faint transistor radios sheltering under plywood and zinc. It was the new alien lord, vexed at the many prayers being offered up to stop its impending romp.

Chapter 41

Ocho Rios

Darlene and Epifanie were like blood sisters. They both arrived in Riverton City with a bump. Darlene called her baby Leon, after the baby's father. He disappeared after she told him she was pregnant. She had an uncle that captured a small plot next Madda Tee. Darlene love to talk about her dancing job and that she made money every night. She told Epifanie that she danced in nice bathing suits that her boyfriend gave to her. Epifanie would try them on when Madda Tee was not around. "God no want to see you batty," she would say.

Moses didn't talk to Darlene unless Epifanie was around. Ever since they were children, Epifanie and Moses shared stories about wormy mangoes, duppy, Blackheart Man and rolling calf. Epifanie stayed inside with Kundu and Darlene would join her with her son Leon. They would take turns watching each other's child. Moses walked with a dozen or more gruff boys about his age, with his friend Makka Beard. They grabbed handbags and food from unsuspecting shoppers at the market and sometimes in the Uptown Plaza. On the third instance of his arrest, the police inspector asked Moses why he couldn't live up to his name.

"Moses is supposed to lead people, not live off them. You more like parasite," the Inspector admonished.

He told Moses that he would call him 'Junjo' from this point on: he was an ugly tainted fungus that eats through precious hard dough bread. It spoils everything.

Moses like the name Junjo. He didn't go to church anyway. Madda Tee told him that her son's name is Moses, not Junjo; she not having any Junjo in her yard. Soon after Junjo left the yard for good, Epifanie left for Ocho Rios. She left crying through the gate and through the muddy road into the darkness of the Riverton City stench. Epifanie walked through the peenie wallies that hovered and lit up the pitch blackness of the road. The smell of burning dry hair and smoke rails lightly against the rotting citrus delivery from the last dump truck.

Darlene told Epifanie to ask for her Uncle Bunny. He runs the Four Score Bar, next to where the Ocho Rios bus makes its final stop before coming back to Kingston. Bunny walked with his head leaning forward and slightly bent at the hip. Even with this adjustment, Bunny had to bend even further to avoid hitting his head on most doorways. He had eight or nine creases in his forehead depending on how annoyed he was. Below his creased forehead were two fiercely piercing eyes that showed red veins scattered around infinitely dark pupils. Jamaican regulars called him 'Lenky' because he was tall and thin; he tells tourists to call him 'Bunny.' He spoke with a whisper, even over loud music. The bar opens at 4pm every day except Sundays. Sunday nights were officially closed, except for the eight to fifteen men that would meet to gamble and play dominoes. Only special tourists knew about Sundays.

Bunny also owned the three-room attachment at the back of the bar. He told Epifanie she could use Darlene's old room in the back. Rent was three times more than Kingston and Mobay. Half her pay plus light and water would come out of her wages every month. Epifanie could call him 'Uncle' like Darlene.

He would take care of her, like his niece. Bunny asked Epifanie if she had ever danced before, or if she had ever talked to a white man. Epifanie said yes, even though she had never done either.

He told her she would meet a lot of customers from Canada and the US. She was pretty and they would buy her a lot of drinks. Most of them just want to talk, he said. Men get a little lonely and need a pretty gyal to make them forget. Because she was a light-skinned woman, she should put on the red bikini top and red leather mini skirt he put on her bed. Uncle Bunny told her she would make a lot of money if she knew how to be nice.

After banana, sugar cane and bauxite, the tourism industry was the fastest growing industry in Jamaica. Boats of tourists fleeing the cold climate of the northeast United States and Europe flock to the island ports to buy trinkets and get pampered in ways they could only imagine. With this new traffic also came Quaaludes, cocaine and LSD. Small taverns, bars and guest houses became dark places where any service would be performed at request. Go-go night clubs were popular with both men and women tourists, looking for the forbidden and sometimes, the innocent.

Epifanie's only sin was with Moses. They did it to ward off the Blackheart Man. It worked. The Blackheart Man never came for Epifanie. Makka Beard stole a quick kiss once, but it enraged Junjo. She dreamed of saving enough money to get Kundu from Riverton City, and the stink that it left pressed into your skin.

She didn't cry when Uncle Bunny showed her how to please a man. He made her stare in his eyes and tell him how handsome he was. Every man wants to hear how good they look, he said. We have to keep them coming back, he said. Talk to them, make them buy drinks. Laugh and smile even when you don't understand the joke. Everything is funny. Everybody is interesting. We going to change your name, make it shorter. Tell them you name 'Pifanie'. 'Epifanie' sound like church. The work would be easy if she had some liquor in her, maybe even a little dust or sugar. After one month, she could listen to a man talk without being in her own body.

She would stand outside herself while she was talking and laughing with a loud British musician from Birmingham. They sat on the bar stool, but Epifanie was a hollow shell. His four-ringed hand rests slightly on her knee. He shouted about Liverpool and beating Tottenham Hotspur. Uncle Bunny was behind the bar, smiling agreeably as if he, too, was enamored with Liverpool.

Later that night, as she told the loud Brit how handsome he was, her mind wandered to the last image of Kundu in her arms. She wondered if anyone would ever tell him how handsome he was. Would she be the only one? As she lay focused on the Brit, projecting a smile, she thought of the money she owed Uncle Bunny and how it left nothing to send to her baby boy Kundu.

Chapter 42

I Di Trinity

The whipping and fanning of rainwater suddenly stops. The weatherman from Radio Jamaica says Hurricane Allan kill at least a thousand people all over the Caribbean. The Dominican Republic get it bad, Haiti even worse. Everything bad always happen to Haiti. It's as if White God don't like them.

The radio announcer says that this is the calm before the storm. Everybody should lock up themselves. A prayer service with hymns struggles through the battery-powered transistor radios. It is 5am says the announcer, echoing above and through the quietness. The unpaved muddy trail is layered with water, mud, gravel, garbage from the dump hills and slabs of useless broken concrete. The last dump truck that passed through the lanes came from a construction site.

There was no old bread, dented cans of soup, open bags of flour, brown lime or even dark sugar to scrape off the ground from this truck. The driver was the skinny man with the big straw hat and the gold chains. His Thames truck was loud as usual, and belched smoke that sounds like a heavy animal snoring.

Coronation Market was closed. The causeway that runs past Riverton City, taking people to the countryside farm areas or in the other direction to downtown Kingston is lifeless, but for the stray dogs and pieces of unidentifiable garments. Three dozen men in the back of four pickup trucks and others in three cars force their way through the muddy water, between the barbed wire and zinc fences. They stop at Standpipe and block the main path leading to the tall dumps. The men have young, underfed bodies but boyish gaunt faces. Some wore shoes, others didn't. White squall hung from the side of their lips. Their eyes were red and desperate. They moved out into the three lanes that led from Standpipe towards the high dumps.

Trinity and about thirty of the agitated men and boys walk down the center lane and the others spread out across the next two. They walk down the lane with black Chopper machine guns and revolvers in hand. Two men have M16s. Trinity has a machete the length of his leg. It shimmers from the early morning sun striking the blade and reflecting on the water, now flowing from the dump heap.

He's tall, with wild bloodshot eyes but no eyebrows on his face or hair on his head. His head has scabs from ringworms and stitched scars from front center, then curves to the left and ends at the back of his head. He's wearing tailored green pants and a black buttoned shirt. On his feet are a pair of black Chinese karate slippers.

"A weh di buoy Junjo deh?" shouts Trinity. "A come we come fi you. Now you a hide like puss weh fraid a dog. Come out nuh!" He slaps his machete on Madda Tee's fence, now partially torn and flattened in the mud. The gunmen behind him spread out into the lifeless yards, including Madda Tee's.

"Tell the batty buoy say him fi come suck him madda before mi chop har up. A talk bout him a don. Don for where? A mi run dis. A Laborite run dis. Bout you a don?" Trinity walks into Madda Tee's yard and stands in front of Madda Tee's door. Kundu looks with one eye through the space between the plywood door and the concrete wall of the single room. Madda Tee waves her hand and points to the floor.

Trinity walks away from the door and calls to the two men carrying the M16 over their shoulders. Kundu lays flat on the cardboard bed next to Lorraine. Madda Tee gestures to Lorraine to keep her head down in the cardboard. The room was quiet and fresh with the smell of rainwater on cinder blocks. The transistor radios in the lane are off.

There is a dull knock across Madda Tee's yard. Madda Tee, Kundu and Lorraine look at each other as Darlene's voice rises above the sound of their shallow breathing. Kundu crawls over to the door and tilts his head to see through the crease between the wall and the door. Lorraine crawls over to the door and looks under Kundu's head. Darlene is standing in front of her door. The loose zinc hanging by one nail slaps the side of her little block room without a sound. Trinity walks up to Darlene and grabs her by the collar with one hand, pulling her down into the mud. He has his glimmering machete in the other hand. A young boy with a black pistol, and neck crowded with silver chains runs over and kicks her in the back, then steps back. Trinity looks back at him and he takes another step back. Rain begins to fall again. It moves quickly across the zinc roofs, popping like bullets. It drops heavier and heavier until it sounds like one big continuous explosion.

Leon rushes out of the room and swings his fist at Trinity, but misses. Trinity lets go of Darlene and she stands up slowly. Leon stands with his legs apart in a horse stance, like the shaolin fighters. He bends his knees and holds up the crane fist. The young boy with the pistol walks from behind Trinity and stands in front of Leon. Trinity turns and walks away, stepping over Madda Tee's barbed wire and zinc fence that is partially covered in mud and water. Kundu, Lorraine and Madda Tee are looking through the crease of the door.

"Lay down flat, no look out deh," says Madda Tee in a loud whisper above the noisy roof.

Looking through the hole, Kundu whispers desperately, "Leon out there."

"Call him," urges Lorraine.

The boy with the black pistol raises his arm and points it at Leon. Darlene jumps in front of Leon, pushing him into the mud and water. They both fall as the smoke from the pistol rises through the pellets of rain. The echo of a dull pop rings through the noise of the rain on zinc. The boy with the pistol turns and follows Trinity's path out of Madda Tee's yard.

Darlene and Leon lay still in the mud as the rain beats ferociously.

Kundu runs out, followed by Lorraine and Madda Tee. Darlene's arm is stretched across Leon. She looks up and around her, then pulls Leon's shoulder. Kundu and Lorraine crash onto their knees into the growing puddle of water. Darlene rolls Leon onto his back; his cut jean shorts and mud brown marina quickly grows red as the rain beats into the ground. He is looking up at Kundu and Lorraine as Darlene covers the hole in his chest. Madda Tee falls to her knees next to Darlene. Leon is taking deep long breaths.

"Mi can't see. Water in my eye," croaks Leon.

Lorraine wipes his face with her shaking hands.

"Lawd have mercy. Jesus Christ," calls out Madda Tee.

Darlene is wailing. "Whoeeeeee."

Kundu holds Leon's hand as Darlene rocks him in her arms, and Madda Tee and Lorraine surround him like a giant leaf shielding him from the rain.

"A dead mi a dead?" says Leon as he chokes up blood.

"Oh, merciful Father, don't take this little boy yah. Him no do nothing Father," prays Madda Tee.

Darlene cries, "Mi son, mi son. Mi one son."

Leon stops moving. His eyes are open, but his chest is still. Darlene stretches herself across him. His body stiffens and then stops.

Lorraine puts her hand on his shoulder. She leans over and sings in his ear.

"We are one in the Spirit
We are one in the Lord
We are one in the Spirit
We are one in the Lord
And we'll pray that our unity
Will one day be restored
And they'll know we are Christians by our love
By our love
And they'll know we are Christians by our love."

Kundu's red and purple eyes flicker with tears as he kneels by Leon. They were the same age, born in the same yard, the same month. He didn't know his father either. They decided that they were more likely to be brothers or maybe cousins. Kundu wipes his eyes and buries his contorted face into his hands.

Rapid machine gunfire, followed by single shot returns, echoing from the yard across from Madda Tee. Dark shadows move quietly and quickly down the lane. The wind has grown stronger and has now forced itself through Darlene's door. It rips off a sheet of zinc from Ms. V's little house. The sheet of zinc flies into the darkened sky and disappears among the other violently unidentifiable flying things.

"We have to go inside." says Madda Tee.

"Mi not leaving him. Whoeee, mi son. Leon," she wails as she rocks him in her arms. Kundu rocks back and sits on his heels, covered in mud. Leon's light grip on his hand melts away.

Darlene screams at the sky and rain.

Chapter 43

Hurricane Allan

Condensed milk cans and pieces of furniture fly high into the dark rain. Rotten fruit and spoiled ground provisions roll and float down from the latest dump delivery. The radios that reported the thousand people that died in Haiti and the Dominican Republic were all off. Batteries have gone low or completely out. The cricket match at Sabina Park was called off five days ago. The Prime Minister issued a State of Emergency order forbidding all travel throughout the country.

Police, fire and lifesaving personnel would be scarce due to the conditions of the road, he said. Police from Harman Barracks and soldiers from Castleton will be on patrol to curtail looting and lawless behavior. As he spoke to the country via Radio Jamaica and the Jamaica Broadcasting Company, supermarkets were sold out of bread, milk, mackerel, sardine, flour, rice, chicken back, pumpkin, kerosene oil, butter, callaloo and matches. The Radio Jamaica daily segment asked everyone to pray for forgiveness.

The pastor said Jamaica had moved away from God. There would be a penance to pay for the short skirts and loose behavior. God did not like the foul language and violent music young people listen to endlessly. People stop going to church, he said. God didn't like the prevalent sex out of wedlock. God was upset about man sleeping with man, women playing the fool with other women. If you look what happen to Haiti, pure destruction. Thou shall not worship any other God but me. But people in Haiti deep into the voodoo. They worship Satan every day. That's why God don't like them. You don't realize every time something bad happen, it happens to them. Jamaica can't go down that road. If you get on your knees now, Jesus will beg the Father to forgive your sins, your transgressions.

The radio station signed off after the word 'transgressions' lingered in the airwaves. The rain started almost the same time that the radio pastor's words ripped through the radios in cars, shops and hurriedly closing stores.

Rainwater is violent. It moves garbage piles that stood burning and rotting in the sun for years. The dump cones were flatter; wood, sheet rock, furniture and glass piles were now collapsing. Through the pinging pop rain, unsynchronized bellowing thuds of car parts, heavy furniture, uprooted trees, and stone walls of concrete erupt between the walls of the Sandy Gully. Water speeds through like a car on a freeway. It bores through noisily, dragging everything it touches into an abyssal darkness. The water is only six feet from the top of the retaining wall. The bomb-like explosions grow more frequent and resonant.

Makka Beard is sitting on the retainer wall. He sits steadily with his shoeless feet hanging over the wall above the rising and contemptuous black water. He's wearing blue jeans cut at the knee, and his locks are dripping water.

Makka Beard's tarpaulin is tied to the fence separating the Sandy Gully from the Riverton dump. Water rushes from the dump next to the fence and splashes against the outer side of the wall where Makka Beard sits. The fire pit and pots he used to cook are all gone. He watches as a fully formed tree spins and twirls rapidly in the water, then it spirals and disappears. Soon after, a light-colored umbrella, still open, bobs up and down next to a rimless tire. They appear to waltz together, vanishing under the strength of the Sandy current.

A yellow Volkswagen Bug bobs and turns down the gully with its lights on. It rolls and bangs into the walls from side to side. The wheels spin as it rolls through the ferocious dark water. Makka Beard stands, and steps down from the wall. The black water whips and turns the Volkswagen upright as if it was driving down the gully on its own. Makka Beard squints at the sight of a small white dog, trapped and pressed against the back window. The driver and passenger windows are closed. The Volkswagen brushed, then banged into the wall, then crosses over to the other side and crashes into the wall again and again.

In the dump mound next to the fence and retaining wall, everything whistled, everything trembled. Makka Beard plods through the migrating insipid water that reeks of rot and decay. He wraps his tarpaulin around himself, tightens his fingers into the holds of the goat fence, and sits down.

Chapter 44

Don Gargon

S atan and his wife a fight, old timers would say. Every time the sun comes through the heavy cloud, the old people with their wrinkled eyelids and mash mouth, would mumble about Satan and how he and his curvaceous wife were locked in a death match over good and evil. No one could prove that Satan's wife, if one existed, would object to evil.

The thought prevailed in Riverton City as the heavy clouds seem to let the sunlight roam through the lanes and into some of the shack houses, now stripped of their roofs. Square, exposed cinder blocks, soaked from horizontal rain, stood waiting for another blow of wind to level everything into the dark quicksand of garbage, waste and mud. The sliver of light exposed the faceless heads running through the lanes, sometimes knocking on a door, sometimes firing rapid shots. Trinity and his Shadow Posse, almost forty men and man-boys, crouch and scamper like hungry dogs, their heads swiveling side to side, up and down. Trinity and thirty of his Shadow Posse walk between the three high dumps filled with mostly broken bottles and tin cans, with the other ten or so seeming to disappear.

The people from Riverton City never climb them to dig for useful garbage. Those that did, returned with deep gashes requiring stitches at the Kingston Public Hospital. The KPH is the only hospital in Kingston that would not charge for treatment. It was only a half-hour bus ride. The ambulance doesn't come to Riverton City unless the police escort them in under protection.

A short man-boy from the Shadow Posse standing in front of Trinity covers his eye and falls to his knees, screaming. Sparks of gunfire from the top of the broken bottle dumps join the beating of rain. Four more Posse members fall to the muddy water. More flashes of fire erupt from behind, crashing into the bottle dump. Trinity takes a gun from the screaming man-boy, now bleeding from his eye. Trinity fires at the top of the dump hill. A shotta comes rolling down the dump hill followed by an avalanche of broken glass. Two more shottas come rolling down the hill, firing their Chopper machine guns randomly into the air, on the ground and into the dump hill. They crash to the ground, into the pool of water and splintered shrapnel. Spits of fire from guns, now in a circle, cut through the Posse.

Trinity lays on top of the man-boy that got shot in the eye. He rolls the boy's body onto his and lays still. Pieces of broken glass from beer and coke bottles sink into his back and neck. Bullets rip into the bodies already laying still in a watery slow flow of blood. The gunfire stops, and the shottas walk slowly down from the three dump mountains of broken bottles and glass. The space between the bases of the three dumps formed a kill circle. The bodies, some thin, some thick, some long and others stubby, sunk halfway into the mud and water. The wind roars like a voice in a conch shell. The bodies are limp, some still smoking from the bullets lodged in cold skin. Junjo walks into the circle as seven shottas inspect the bodies by kicking the feet.

Trinity is covered with the lifeless body he used as a shelter. Beneath the muddy water, now blackened with thick blood,

Trinity grips his long machete. A shotta pulls the body of the dead man-boy off of Trinity. Steady heavy rain beats down into Trinity's face. He opens his eyes and swings his machete across his body. The blade cuts though the jaw and teeth of the shotta and he falls to his knees. Trinity stands up.

"Hol' on! No shoot him, no shoot him. Him no have no gun," shouts Junjo.

The shotta next to Trinity is still on his knees and then falls face first into the muddy water, chased with his own blood.

"Mi no have nothing on me but this," says Trinity, holding out his machete. His back and neck are bleeding through his clothes. He swings his machete again, striking the head and neck of the shottas already down in the bloody mud pool.

"Hol' on, hol' on," screams Junjo to the shottas.

"Kill him bomboclaat," interjects Baby Face Shotta.

"No! Hol' on man." Junjo points to Baby Face Shotta. "I want to do this myself. Is me you come for, right? What you name?" demands Junjo.

"I a Trinity, Father, Son, Holy Ghost. My bredda you kill. If you no puss, we can deal with the case. You see me." Trinity takes a step over the dying shotta.

"A oh," says Junjo and sucks his teeth. The wind blows the shottas back and forth, and pushes them in a circle. A puff of smoke streaks out into the air along with a pop. Baby Face Shotta lowers his gun, then puts it in his waist. Junjo looks over at him quizzically, then looks back at Trinity who's now on his knees. A small hole is in his forehead. He falls backward into the pool of mud, water and blood. The shottas continue to kick the bodies and collect their weapons and ammunition.

"Meet me a di yard in a half hour." Junjo barks at Baby Face Shotta, then walks over to him. "Next time me tell you fi do something mek sure you do it. I have some questions for him. How we going to know how much man them have, when them a come? Meet me a the yard. Tell the man dem fi look out. Them have more people at Standpipe. Go deal with that first, and then come check me." Baby Face Shotta raises his chin and walks away towards the shottas checking the bodies.

Chapter 45

Rain a Fall, Breeze a Blow

Jomo, like other abandoned dogs, slinks and cowers under the single room shacks that were fortunate to be built on stilts. Jomo settled under Peta-Gaye's old shack. Her father left Riverton soon after her funeral. He never spoke to anyone, and for that matter, he never really spoke again.

His daughter was torn apart by an animal no one can seem to find. Pastor Beloved prayed for him, and even gave him a little something from the offering bag. Peta-Gaye's father cleared out his little square room and left Jomo standing by the open door. The cinder block square shack was for anyone who wanted it. No one had gone to plunder or claim it yet. Jomo lived there.

He was short, white with spots, huge wide jaws, and a head too big for his body, and a short stubby tail.

Peta-Gaye named him after Jomo Kenyatta of Kenya. Lorraine and Peta-Gaye wanted to be freedom fighters like Jomo and Nanny of the Maroons. Lorraine wanted to free people and teach them how to fight back.

The water from the rain had risen two feet now, and the houses on stilts, with the space at the bottom had nowhere for anyone to hide, not even a dog. Joncrow birds, normally flying with giant wings across the sky, surveying the dead and those soon to be dead, hunker under accidental shelters atop the dump piles. They clutch their wings close to their body to avoid taking flight. The wind would take them anyway, pitching them down the dump hill until they catch something that supports their claws. Up and down, they go, fighting to keep the makeshift shelter they only discovered by falling.

Madda Tee, Kundu, Lorraine and Ms. V sit in a circle on Kundu's refrigerator cardboard bed. The flame from the kerosene lamp is desperate to stay alive. They stared at each other without talking.

Kundu and Lorraine had helped Darlene carry Leon into her little room. They gently placed him on her box frame and covered him with a bed sheet from his toes to his neck as if he was sleeping. Darlene sat next to him, then covered him with her body. She groaned and twisted, her back and head shivered and convulsed. Darlene violently vomits, then falls lifeless onto Leon's lifeless chest. Lorraine and Kundu follow Madda Tee back to the struggling kerosene lamp in her room. Ms. V sat motionless with her eyes closed, whispering prayers.

A loud bang shakes the room, then a scraping sound. They all jump and look at each other.

"Sound like mi roof gone," says Ms. V.

"How you know?" asked Madda Tee.

"It was a shake and tremble from before."

"My own next. A it this?"

Water is seeping through the walls. The box bed is soft and damp. The Dutch pot and spoons in the corner of the room shake and rattle as a stronger wind surrounds the house. Kundu's belly growls loudly. He hadn't eaten since the day before.

"Look yah. You and Lorraine go up to the church." says Madda Tee.

"But --" protests Kundu.

"Mi not asking you. You hear me?" snaps Madda.

Kundu nods his head.

"Go up to the church, you and Lorraine. Tell Pastor say you hungry and you house a blow way. Them have food a the church. Plus the church build stronger that this place yah. A come this ya storm a come fi tek we."

"Mi wi stay with you," says Ms V. to Madda Tee.

"Stay with me for what? Nothing no wrong with you foot. This foot not taking me up that hill. Look how them swell." Madda Tee moves her feet closer to the light.

Ms. V. laughs. "Your foot and my eye dem. You can't walk and I can't see. Don't get old. Bible say once a man, twice a child." Ms. V is pointing at Kundu and Lorraine.

Lorraine sits staring through the crevice between the wall and the door. The blood from Leon was all gone now. The water swooshes back and forth, crashing into the outhouse and Darlene's wet cement wall. The place where Leon lived was dark. The half-open door, mangled by the wind, exposed a lifeless darkness that once spoke of rolling calf and kung fu. Kundu was looking in the same place too. His purple eyes released clear fingernail-sized drops of water.

"A it this Father? Oh God, oh God. Pass this cup no. The little pickney them, them no live fi see nothing Father God, merciful Father. In your name I pray, oh God," whispers Madda Tee. "Father up in heaven hallowed be thy name, thy kingdom come, thy will be done upon this earth." She looks up as water begins to spew at the corner of her roof.

"Them can't leave now." Ms. V. shakes her head.

"Them have to wait until the eye," warns Madda Tee. "When the eye come everything going to stop. A so hurricane and storm go. You hear them talk about the eye of the storm.,"

"This here hurricane is a different something," exclaims Ms. V. "You no here them say a the biggest hurricane in the history of the world. Mercy God!"

The water has come flowing up the slight grade and under Madda Tee's door. It moves in and out like waves from a spirited ocean. Kundu's cardboard bed was soaked through. The water is warm and sparkles under the light from the kerosene lamp, which stood like a lighthouse surrounded by water and darkness.

Chapter 46

She a Dream

Before she left for Ocho Rios, Darlene showed Epifanie how to dance like a go-go dancer. She showed her how to make little circles with her hips and lick her lips like she was tasting a ripe, juicy mango, fresh off the tree. Darlene showed Epifanie how to bubble up and down and taste her little finger. Epifanie laughed and giggled when they practiced. Darlene told her everything about the go-go dance, but she never told her about Uncle Bunny.

Uncle Bunny showed all the go-go performers how to dance for the American men, how to laugh for the English men or Australian men. Uncle Bunny showed all the dancers how to make the men drink and order the more expensive fish and liquor.

He would show Epifanie himself how to be a popular hostess and go-go girl. He taught Darlene, too. When Darlene started showing her bump, he put her on a train to Kingston. He promised to help her settle into a nice place in Vinyard Town. After two months and no money, a woman from the Salvation Army told her about a woman that passed away, leaving a one-room house in the middle of the garbage collection land. There was too much shame to go home to her mother and confess that her baby's father is her mother's oldest brother. She moved into the abandoned one-room brick house. There, she had Leon. He came screaming in the darkness and the stale stench of the Riverton City night.

Epifanie was still small and slender. She was light-skinned, like brown sandpaper. Uncle Bunny taught her how to use her eyes, mouth, hands, and everything she owned. She started dancing seven days per week. Her picture was glued to the wall outside the club. Uncle Bunny soon asked her to meet with special customers. They were stressed, he said, she should be nice. He would arrange for meetings in the room he rented to her. All the men were stressed white men who loved disco music, and black girls that loved to laugh and dance. They especially like the black women who liked being kissed, too. After a year, Epifanie stopped dancing completely. She stayed in her room and answered the door for the loud Australian. Sometimes it was the American investor that loved to touch her hair. He was from California. He liked his fun from a needle, he told Epifanie. There was a stinging pain at first. Then it disappeared. Epifanie would fall in and out of dreams, floating to far places.

Uncle Bunny would give her a sample when she needed it to quiet the shaking. She would make enough to pay her rent and the floating dreams.

She never made friends with the other go-go girls. Uncle Bunny kept her as his prize hen, murmured the other dancers. Epifanie loved her period; she could rest. Uncle Bunny said nobody wanted to see a dutty gyal. Epifanie never left the club. He bought her panties and brassiere, lip gloss, earrings and tampons. When she closed her eyes, she couldn't remember Kundu's face beneath the weight of the bloated Australian. Her spirit wailed under the grunt and sweat of faceless hair and freckled skin.

Chapter 47

Quiet Storm

The rain and wind had stopped suddenly. It was exactly the way Madda Tee said it would happen. Half of Madda Tee's roof was gone. A small pool of rainwater rocks from side to side on Kundu's cardboard bed.

Ms. V's little room was blown over into rubble. Her clothes and shoes she kept in the corner of the room were gone. The blocks lay cracked and detached from the cement that held them together. It crumbled. The fence that separated the yards from the driving path for the parade of dump trucks was gone without a trace. The hood of a red car pushed out from the mud and water next to the outhouse. The outhouse door was gone. The water buckets used to take a shower were also gone.

Madda Tee told Kundu and Lorraine to hurry before the eye of the storm passes. She said the back part of the hurricane, after the eye, worse. Kundu looks back at Madda Tee and Ms. V as he and Lorraine step past the shaking plywood door. They step suspiciously into the muddy water past where the fence once stood and start running up the main path reserved for the trucks. As they splash through the water and sludge, they step over razor-sharp can lids, cracked bottles, branches from sugar cane trees, plastic wrappers, dirty diapers, bicycle wheels, and dead dogs.

They run past Jomo's gate, but he doesn't chase after them. The house that Peta-Gaye's father left behind was not captured yet, due to the hurricane. Allan did not take the roof. The bricks were all in place. Lorraine's gaze lasted over ten steps. She reminisces in vivid images of Peta-Gaye running out to walk with her to school. They would certainly dodge the big wheel trucks that started offloading at 4am. Lorraine thought for a moment of the poem they had to learn for the annual end of year recital. How Peta-Gaye would always forget the first part, and Lorraine would forget the last part.

Kundu looks back at her then steps over a half of a windshield.

"If we must die," Lorraine mumbles.

"What you say?" asked Kundu. He points to the back of a wooden chair. Its edges, sharp and bone white, were sticking out from under the mud. Lorraine steps around it. "If we must die? What you mean?"

"The poem. Claude McKay. The recital poem. Me and Peta-Gaye recite it."

"Oh." Kundu looks up ahead as water flows over his bare feet, carrying cigarette boxes, plastic forks, bottle caps and pieces of the Sunday Gleaner.

"It says, 'If we must die, let it not be like hogs hunted and penned in an inglorious spot,'" replies Lorraine. "This feel like that to me."

The pop, then thunderous flurry of gunshots slice through the eerie silence. It stops, then starts again. Kundu and Lorraine turn into a side lane where the pathway is just a little more than shoulder wide. They crouch below the height of the reshuffled zinc fences. Some were flat on the ground and others were mushed into each other like vines. Kundu sees a woman standing outside the door of an elevated brick house with a light flickering through the half-open door. Rapid shots blare, popping on zinc and whizzing through the air above Kundu and Lorraine's heads, and they start to run, one behind the other. As they get to the woman standing outside the house with the flickering light, she waves at them to come inside. Without looking up at her, Kundu and Lorraine run into the house. The woman comes in behind them, as they both crouch in the corner of the house and search for the woman's face.

Horse Mouth Lucy closes the door and bolts three locks at the top, the middle and bottom. She crouches in the middle of the room, taking a deep breath, then blowing out the lamp. Another barrage of gunshots, this time cracking further away, retort in earnest as desperate feet run through the narrow lane. The room was dark as to imagine death.

Kundu and Lorraine are breathing heavily after running harder than they've ever had to. No one made a sound, as heavy footsteps splash right outside the door. The splash of footsteps stop. Suddenly the banging of knuckles against the wood door jolts through the silence of deep breathing from Kundu and Lorraine. Horse Mouth Lucy didn't make a sound; she didn't breathe.

They all sit quietly in the dark. Kundu and Lorraine sit shoulder to shoulder, their knees pulled up to their chest, looking for Horse Mouth Lucy's face through the darkness.

"Sshheeee!" Horse Mouth Lucy whispers.

The darkness is still thick. More footsteps splash through the narrow lane. A man's voice shouts something muffled, then a single shot. There's a rumble of feet and grunts stampeding through the darkness. A high-pitched voice howls like a dog hit with a rock, but then becomes muffled after another single shot.

"Them gone," says Horse Mouth Lucy. The smell of kerosene oil dominated the room. Another aroma lingered above the kerosene, like burned wood and partially burned animal hair. Coming from the ground, seeping into the kerosene is the smell of diarrhea and rum vomit.

Horse Mouth Lucy stands up in the darkness and walks over to the corner across from the children. Lorraine strains her eyes to find where the footsteps lead. They can see each other now. Kundu's knee cut jeans expose his scabs from scrapes climbing the pile. He climbed every day to look for bamboo wood to make his kite. His greying t-shirt that reads 'Harbor Shark' on the front, has moth holes around the neck and shoulders. Lorraine remains crouched in the corner of the room. She's wringing out the bottom of her blue nurse's uniform that reads 'KPH' on the front, and straightens out her thigh-long black PE shorts. Her mix-matched tennis shoes are covered in mud. They used to be white.

Horse Mouth Lucy strikes a match and the yellow light reveals her face from across the room. Kundu and Lorraine watch her intently as they both recognize her at the same time. She has on a long white dress that drags on the floor as she walks. Her hair was wrapped in a white cloth matching her dress. A red sash was tied around her small waist. Her arms and neck are covered, but her form was defined.

"Is the obeah woman." whispered Lorraine to Kundu.

"Who tell you me a obeah woman? You father?" asked Horse Mouth Lucy.

Lorraine and Kundu gazed steadily into her wrinkled face. The light from the match illuminated her darkened pupils. She smiled, then grinned, exposing her bright white teeth across her wide mouth.

"My name is not obeah woman. Call me Ms. Lucy." She bends her knees and squats before the kerosene lamp in the center of the room. She lights the wick and it crackles, then throws a ball of light across the room and casts Horse Mouth Lucy's giant shadow against the ceiling. The light reveals elastic sealed plastic bags around the edge of the room. Little bags stacked on top of each other. The wall behind her was painted red, showing a goat's head. The eyes were holes, with two horns jutting out as if attacking anything standing before it. There is a ring hanging from its nostrils.

"What you doing out here in this storm?" smirked Horse Mouth Lucy.

"We going up to the church," replied Kundu. He sees a bag against the wall shift, but looks again, and nothing happens. "My grandmother send us up there 'cause of the hurricane." Kundu surveys the room closely.

Horse Mouth Lucy shakes her head in disbelief. "You lucky. The Shadow Posse and the Shotta them a fight. You don't hear how much shot a fire? You must love you church bad."

"The church stronger than the house," Lorraine declares.

"Oh. A so? But no same god send hurricane fi come kill we off?" Horse Mouth Lucy peers at Lorraine. "Little girl, how old are you?"

"Twelve. I'm going to be twelve in September."

Horse Mouth Lucy pulls out a handbag from the pile against the wall. She opens it and takes out a silver TV antenna and extends it from twelve inches long to three feet. She draws a circle around the kerosene lamp. She runs the end of the antenna around the circle, until a two-inch-deep groove forms into the dirt.

"How about you?" Horse Mouth Lucy looks at Kundu.

"Twelve."

Horse Mouth Lucy takes the lamp from the center of the circle and puts it against the wall. She draws a square intersecting a triangle, then another circle. "You hungry?" she asked.

Kundu looks over at Lorraine. They both look at the goat head on the wall. The horns are right above Horse Mouth Lucy's head. They stick out from both sides of her head as if they were her own.

"I have some star apples. Them sweet. You have to eat them, 'cause if you don't eat them, they will spoil." Horse Mouth Lucy walks over to the wall next to the locked door and takes out two red star apples. She hands one to Lorraine and the other to Kundu. It has been at least one day since they ate anything, except old Excelsior crackers and salt mackerel from a busted tin.

Kundu takes a bite then Lorraine bites hers; it was sweet and fresh. The white fleshy part of the apple was crunchy but still soft. Kundu and Lorraine bite deeper into the apple. They ate faster, like desperate prisoners at the mercy of their captor. Horse Mouth Lucy's smile presses away the wrinkles she has always had. She digs a smaller circle around the apex of the triangle and the intersection with the square. She digs with a small spoon, removing a half-inch of wet dirt at a time.

"Young girl - Lorraine, right? Your father used to come here. Him say somebody obeah him. And is nothing but bad luck since. A me rub him up with lizard oil. Now him gone a 'Merica a live big. You is a lucky gyal pickney. The girl them that the blackheart man take away go sodomize, them the same age as you. Through you father you lucky." She continues to dig. "And you, Mr. Dundus. Kundu right? I know you from you born. I know you mother and you father."

"You know my mother and father?" asks Kundu. His mouth is partially open with pieces of star apple protruding from his lips. "I don't remember her face," he speaks under his breath.

"You want to know where she is?" Horse Mouth Lucy's eyebrows are arched and curious.

"Where? Kundu has stopped eating.

"Come over here." Horse Mouth Lucy waves at him to come closer. Kundu gets up slowly, then walks on his hands and knees towards the edge of the circle facing Horse Mouth Lucy.

She reaches to her left and pulls out the bag that Kundu thought he saw move. She opens it and takes out a white Croaking lizard. Horse Mouth Lucy gently puts the lizard in the center hole she just dug out. The lizard's tail moves slowly, but stays in the circle. She pours oil on the edge of the big circle, then strikes a match and lights it. The flame races around lightning-fast, eating up the oil in its path until the circle of fire was complete. The white Croaking lizard changed its skin to yellow.

Horse Mouth Lucy stares at Kundu. "Can you do that?"

"What you mean?"

"Change your skin like the lizard. First, he was white, now him yellow. Can you do that?"

"No." Kundu leans away from the circle.

"Albino people have special powers, you know. Yes, everything about you is special. You eye, you blood, even your sweat have power. Let me see you hand."

Lorraine stands up slowly, staring at the lizard in the middle of the circle. Kundu sits on his knees and extends his hand to Horse Mouth Lucy.

"You know my mother?" asks Kundu again.

"Yes, I was here when she have you. If I did know say you was a Dundus, I would a take some of the after birth for me self." Everybody think say you a white man pickney. Your mother, Epifanie, lucky, lucky bad! She have a powerful son."

Lorraine crouches in front of the door.

"I just want a little drop of your power, so I can help people with sickness," Horse Mouth Lucy continues. "You want to help people, right? Me just want a little bit." She grips Kundu's hand and pulls him closer to her.

"You know where she live?" Kundu pulls back slightly.

Horse Mouth Lucy takes a small folding knife from her sash. She opens the knife, holding it with one hand and pulling out the blade with her bright white fence teeth. She plunges the knife into the lizard, then places it in the palm of Kundu's hand. Lorraine pushes Horse Mouth Lucy into the circle of fire. Kundu jumps up as Lorraine unlocks the top bolt; she had quietly unlocked the bottom and middle locks. Lorraine ran through the door, jumping into the high water and mud. Kundu jumps out behind her but falls hands first into the water. As they both stood up, a gust of wind blows them to the ground. Heavy sand-like raindrops sting their faces and arms, and it soon whipped their entire bodies. They begin to run back towards the main lane. Allan's eye had passed, and now everything suddenly had wings.

Chapter 48

Gurty a Foreign

Madda Tee and Ms. V sit shoulder to shoulder in the corner of the room against the wall. The cinder blocks weren't moving, though water seeped through, discoloring the light grey into a darker shade. Everything in the room was wet now. Ms. V mumbled scriptures in a secret language, like the children in Sunday service that didn't quite learn the passage or knew how to read.

Swirls of wind would find its way into the room, whipping Madda Tee and Ms. V further into the corner, next to Madda Tee's clothes barrel. The barrel held all her clothes, dolls, birth certificates, pictures, and letters. The birth certificate and letters were kept in a plastic bag at the top. Madda Tee pressed up against the barrel, and Ms. V against her, while more sand-like rain beats against the uneven gravel floor.

Two months earlier, Madda Tee picked up a letter from the post office. She had to use her birth certificate to prove she was Ms. Thompson, and that she lives near Standpipe in the squatters' village people call 'Riverton City.' Ms. V had to co-sign for the letter. Ms. V had a driver's license she paid for through a Justice of the Peace. The letter was from Ms. Gurty. Madda Tee hadn't heard from her little sister since she sent the one barrel of clothes, many years ago. Madda Tee couldn't believe that her little sister would treat her like dirty water used to wash clothes. She was quietly heartbroken but never complained to anyone. She would always tell anyone who would listen that Gurty married a man that look like Jesus. Madda Tee announced that Gurty would send for her to join her in America almost every day. When the letter came, Madda Tee had Ms. V open and read it to her. Madda Tee complained that she can't make out the writing and that Gurty always write like doctor.

Dear Heart, how you do? A long time we no talk, me no see you. Every day a wonder how you do, how the sugar, and blood pressure. Your foot them still swell up? How you manage with the walking?

I couldn't even talk before now because me a run and hide like thief.

Dear Heart it no easy over here. How Kundu? Him big now. What going on with Moses and Epifanie? Tell Moses say to behave himself.

Make me tell you, me run left the white man. We broke up. Him a try beat me, But me not taking no beating from nobody. The man drink like fish. Everyday him stink a rum.

As soon as my paper come in the mail, I jump on a bus to Miami. I know people over there, so a here I live now.

I get a certificate in cosmetology, so now I can do hair. Rent a room in the back of a Jamaican woman I know from Mo Bay.

She say she know papa. She talk about how she and Big Leaf a friend from Primary school. The world small, right? So a her house me rent room in a. A tell her a sending for you. I will pay the little extra rent.

There is a boat leaving Kington Harbor August 30th. The name of the ship is Scirroco. Is the same Captain that I use to deal with. Him still like me, but I still pay him to carry you up here.

I don't know what you going to do about Kundu. Maybe you should send him to Epifanie. Them only have the one space on the ship. Call Epifanie to come for him.

Make sure say you get to the ship by 4 in the morning.

A love you, Dear Heart. A see you soon.
Gurty

When Ms. V finished reading the letter to Madda Tee, she folded it and carefully placed it back into the envelope it came. Madda Tee placed it in a plastic bag. She would present it as her ticket to stow away.

Chapter 49

Our Angel

Parts and sometimes entire sheets of zinc fences fly through the air, cutting through the darkness like razor blades. There is a story of a brave - or stupid - man that went out to look for his dog during a storm two years ago. He crawled around on his hands and knees in the mud, searching in the small spaces under the shacks built on cinder block stilts. He found the dog, but lost his own head when he stood upright to walk away.

Tonight, Hurricane Allan has lifted every roof, some in sections, others in whole swathes, opening the gates to heavy balls of rain. Seven men from the Shadow Posse, stranded by Trinity's death are walking through a narrow lane towards Standpipe and the main road leaving Riverton City. They half run and walk, ducking under flying unidentifiable objects that appear to drop out from the darkness.

The last man in the back of the seven faceless men falls forward gripping his back. The wind rumbles and roars like thunder. Another man falls, grabbing his knees and crying out faintly. The other five men scramble and fall flat. They begin to fire their guns in every direction into the dark. One man stands up, pointing his machine gun into the sky, then fires in the direction from which they came. Suddenly he falls forward, his machine gun hurling shots into the muddy water. The pops of the gunshots are muffled and dull under the barking of wind and clanking sound of exposed flying metals everywhere. Four men crawl towards the road leading to the highway. Flashing pops of light flicker through the darkness. The men crawling through the floating garbage, anchored in mud and now blood-stained rain, move slower and slower. The shottas walk out of the three lanes that lead to Standpipe. They walk deliberately over the bodies of the men on the ground. They stand over each man and then fire one shot.

"Make sure nobody a move." commands Baby Face Shotta. The shottas move around the bodies again, sometimes shooting once, twice or even three times. Junjo is on one knee next to the water pipe stand. A small car door whips through the darkness and careens into a slender shotta, knocking him onto the ground.

"Make we left ya so!" snarls Baby Face Shotta. He looks over at Junjo, who's still on one knee and holding his rib cage.

"What happen to you?" Junjo's brown marina shirt is turning red. Baby Face Shotta is surprised. "You get shot?"

"Carry me go a Lucy. She know what to do." Junjo grunts and exhales heavily.

"Boss get lick. We a go carry him to the obeah woman," calls out Baby Face Shotta to the others.

The shottas gather around Junjo, raising his arms around their shoulders, crouching and drudging through spirited waves of flowing garbage. They travel slowly down the main truck path, away from Standpipe. There are eight shottas now, including Junjo.

The sideway rain beats into their skin and the wind knocks them periodically to the ground. Baby Face Shotta walks ahead of the scrum. He has a machine gun that he picked up from the last Shadow Posse man that pleaded while lying face down in the mud. The shottas quick-stepped through the narrow alley, through cans and bottles popping against sheets of zinc. Spikes from barbed wire fences stick out of the ground. They can pierce through shoes and socks. One shotta yells out after sinking the soft sole of his Hush Puppies into a rusty protruding spike. Another shotta pushed him forward.

They muscle their way through the shoulder wide alleyway until they get to Horse Mouth Lucy's dark, window-less brick house. Baby Face Shotta takes Junjo inside and closed the door behind him. In the room, there were bags strewn out of place and a low circle of fire smoldering in the center back of the room. Horse Mouth Lucy's left hand was wrapped in soft white cotton material. Her white dress was soiled in grease, lizard blood and dirt.

Junjo groans as Baby Face Shotta anchors him down into the corner of the room.

"Him get shot. Him say you have something."

Horse Face Lucy quickly checks Junjo. "Boy, me almost have the wickedest obeah oil. The dundus boy was here. Him and the mawga coolie girl that always behind him and the other one up a Madda Tee."

"Don't trouble him," whispered Junjo.

"If me get one speck of him blood. Dundus blood have power you know," claims Horse Mouth Lucy.

Junjo groans and tries to sit up facing her. "I tell you before, don't trouble him. Leave him out of your obeah business." Junjo closes his eyes and slumps to the side. His head moves up and down as he breathes heavily.

Horse Mouth Lucy pleads. "Him don't understand the power me a talk about. You can't catch disease, not even a cold. If you get shot, you bleed for a little, but you heal quick."

Baby Face Shotta crawls across the room towards him. Junjo's chest and belly roll like waves. Baby Face Shotta takes his handkerchief from around his neck and wraps it around his hand. He held it up to Junjo's face, then covers his mouth and nose. Junjo struggles, and pushes Baby Face Shotta backward, then lunges for him.

Horse Mouth Lucy jumps on Junjo's back and pulls him backward with her arms around his neck, gripping him tight. Baby Face Shotta drives his knee into Junjo's side and covers his nose and mouth again.

They hold Junjo down. His legs move slowly like the tail of the dead lizard. With all three locked into a grip of death, the clapping sound of flying stray wood banging against the wall outside breaks the tension of muscles and bone. They let go of Junjo and his limp body slinks lifelessly into the plastic bags lined up against the wall. Horse Mouth Lucy pushes Junjo's legs closer to the wall and away from her door.

"You have to bring the dundus to me," she commands.

"Morning, we catch him." replies Baby Face Shotta.

"No, tonight. This is the perfect time," insists Horse Face. "Hurricane mean say God and Satan a fight. Him and the coolie gyal Lorraine gone to the church. Madda Tee house must be flat cause of the wind. You know how much power in that boy blood? Bring him back to me. A you run Riverton City now. You don't have to fear nothing."

Chapter 50

Toes in Hell, Fingers in Heaven

"Oh Father God, look after the pickney them. Carry them go a the church, cover them, oh God," prayed Madda Tee. She forces her door shut, after the wind blows it open once more. Ms. V helps her push the barrel in front of the door. Water flows in through the torn roof and sprays them from head to toe. The ground and foundation of the little brick house trembles and sways.

Ms. V closes her eyes. "Pray for Junjo and Epifanie too. I mean Moses. Pray for Moses. Pray the Lord have mercy on them. Especially Moses," says Ms. V. "Remember him used to give us money to spend."

Madda Tee shakes her head. "Blood money! Collect insurance from the people, talking about him a Don."

"But no so it go. If him don't do it, somebody else will do it. And then on top of it, a him used to patrol the street them a night and fight off the Laborite them. No police coming down here unless them declare state of emergency. See the little girl them get capture, rape and cut up, and them come down here for two days. People a look for them own pickney. Them no care."

"How you know say a no him or him shotta boy them no take the girl them?"

"A no them. One of the shotta sister get kidnapped too. Somebody rape and cut her up from her head top to her baby toe. The one them call 'Baby Face', his sister. Every time you see him, him eye them red like him a drink rum all day." Ms. V. pulls Kundu's cardboard closer to her and Madda Tee, forming a short wall against the spraying water squeezing through the exposed roof.

"From the day him call himself Junjo and a go round a beat-up people for their money, and a talk bout him a killer and Don Gargon, I stop calling him my son. I don't raise any murderer. A because him born in a sinful way. Me and di preacher go lay down, and ever since, a nothing but bad luck, and punishment on this earth. Is like we curse. I pray every day. Tell God say me sorry.

"But look, me daughter turn stripper a club for more white people. My son a big murderer. My grandson don't know none of them. When him ask for him mother, I shame bad. I can't even look in him face. See the curse that I put on him. Everywhere him go, somebody a point on him. Call duppy, ghost, dundus and all kind a things. How him going to get a work? When me dead and gone, who a go look on him? Him no have nobody. Jesus Christ! All of this because I make one mistake. Lawd God have His mercy," Madda Tee cries out.

"You son no all bad, Madda Tee." Ms. V rubs her shoulder. "Every week, a him give me money to buy things for Kundu. A him pay for Kundu's school uniform. I always say I have extra money because I work uptown sometimes, but I know say you wouldn't take it if you know Moses give it to me. A him pay for the books for school. I never got lucky and find them. Moses give me the money. I would a say something to you, but I know say you would a fuss. Even, though him a bad man, him never leave out him pickney. Him a move in a silence. Plus if people know say, Kundu was Junjo's son, then, they would take out them bad mind on Kundu. It better off for people not to know."

"Why Junjo? That name. Moses is the Bible hero that save people. Junjo cause bread to rotten and turn green. Nobody can eat Junjo bread." Madda Tee looks over at Ms. V and smiles.

The door blows in slightly again, and they push the barrel closer to the door and push against it with their backs.

Chapter 51

The Beloved

The Church of Deliverance has a flat roof. It is surrounded by old dump hills that started many years before the most recent pile on the opposite end of Riverton City. The opposite end is where the bodies were found. The dump hill separates the church from the fence and the turbulent Sandy Gully.

The gully is known to drag careless people out to sea, never to be seen again. It carries trees, whole houses, dogs, cars, furniture and idle people that love to play foolish games - all out to sea. The dump piles are high above the church, so the winds don't get a chance to grab the roof and shake it like a dog on a bone.

Kundu and Lorraine wobble forward and sideways towards the church. The path is indistinguishable from the start of the piles that once was a clear lane to the doors of the church. The wind was softer. Over many years, the garbage dump became glued together as sturdy as a wall. The door and window of the church is closed, but Kundu and Lorraine could hear singing coming from inside. Kundu walks cautiously behind Lorraine.

The Congregation is singing loudly.

"We are one in the Spirit

We are one in the Lord

We are one in the Spirit

We are one in the Lord

And we pray that our unity will one day be restored

And they'll know we are Christians

By our love

By our love......"

Lorraine and Kundu stand under the awning above the front door. They try the knob but the door is locked; Lorraine knocks on the door. Kundu joins her and they knock again. As the door opens a wave of heat rushes out. The painting of White Jesus Christ hangs looming in the faint light of candles. The choir pit has five kerosene lanterns. The congregation sat on the benches and floor. Pastor Beloved, on his knees next to his pulpit, palms raised to the ceiling, prays vociferously.

"Oh Father God, blessed be Thy name oh Father. Bestow upon us your mercy we pray, Father God.

"We are your children, Father, we worship and exalt in your name. Oh God tomorrow is not promised, oh Father, but we asked for Your mercy Father. Protect us from this hurricane, oh God. We just want to praise Your name, oh God. Make us Your vessel, oh Father. Anoint us with Your heavenly favor oh Lord.

"Cover us and protect us, oh God. Thank you, Jesus, thank you Lord, thank you Father. Everybody say the Lord's Prayer."

One of the twelve church deaconesses that support Pastor Beloved, stands at the door in front of Lorraine and Kundu. The deaconess is round and portly. Her pink gabardine work skirt and jacket struggled to contain her.

"Oh child, what you doing out here?" asks the deaconess.

"The roof tearing off," says Lorraine as a sharp gust of wind opens the door wider. Lorraine and Kundu get forced through the door. The deaconess looks at Kundu, then motions to a man from the choir. The man comes over to the deaconess and she whispers in his ear. He sings solo every Sunday. He's tall with a long, vein-filled neck.

Lorraine and Kundu are drenched; their bare feet are muddy and smattered with fresh cuts and bruises. The choir man inspects them from head to toe.

"You can come in." says the deaconess, pointing at Lorraine and pulling her by the hand.

Kundu looks up at the man from the choir, then takes a step backward.

"Him can't come in?" asks Lorraine.

"We don't have any space. You can stay in that corner over there. Just church members today." says the deaconess.

"I can sit on the floor, right here?" says Kundu, pointing to the corner next to the door.

"Everybody know say dundus bad lucky. We have to close the door."

Kundu steps back. The choir man closes the door. Kundu stands under the awning of the church. He takes a step into the mud and walks away from the church and the pile next to the Sandy Gully. The door of the church springs open and Lorraine comes running into the rain. She taps Kundu on the shoulder.

"Where you going?"

"Don't know. Why you come out?" Kundu replied.

"I don't want hurricane blow you away. If the wind come, I can hold on to your foot."

Kundu wipes the rain from his face and smiles. "What if it pick we up?"

"Me still hold on tight," declares Lorraine. "Not letting you go."

"You the only friend I have."

"Me too."

They both plop their way down the slight hill from the church. The rain slows down to a drizzle and then to soft drops. The wind swirled, and push Lorraine and Kundu into fences, and then deep ruts and gashes covered with water.

"I going back to Madda Tee. She no have nobody."

He hops over low points and steps on high points above the garbage-fermented smell carried by the water. Lorraine is walking on the side of her feet, as she has a fresh cut in the sole of her feet from a condensed milk can.

Like the rain, the wind is slower and only whistles now. Looking down the lane, disjointed fences, once proudly lined with zinc, cinder blocks and barbed wire, lay helplessly covered in mud, migrated garbage, floating feces and dead bloated animals. It's 5:00am. The morning sun is lost behind the clouds, but it flips the cover of night from darkness with a little light, to light with a little darkness.

"Look!" Lorraine points to the shottas emerging from a narrow lane.

"The same one from Aunt Pet's house?" asks Kundu.

Six shottas, led by Baby Face Shotta are walking up the hill towards them. The children turn around quickly and start walking back up the hill. They pass the church as the congregation sings triumphantly;

"Praise my soul the King of heaven;

To His feet Thy tribute bring.

Ransomed, healed, restored, forgiven,

Evermore His praises sing

Alleluia, alleluia

Praise the everlasting King."

Kundu and Lorraine rush up the dump pile. They use both hands and feet in the way Leon would crawl up the steep hill.

The pile is looser than before. The wind and water made it slippery and frightening. Pieces of rotted furniture fall apart and roll down the pile. The shottas are slipping and rolling on the side of the dump hill. Kundu and Lorraine get to the top of the hill and then run down towards the fence to the hole Leon discovered. The old piles connect at the base, forming an artificial mountain ridge. They formed a line blocking the way to the Sandy Gully goat fence and retaining wall. Kundu and Lorraine get to the bottom of the hill and squeeze through the hole that tore Kundu's shirt.

The rain had stopped, but the angry water rocketed through the gully. It screamed like a hungry animal desperate for more food. Kundu and Lorraine run alongside the retaining wall, jumping over garbage from the pile. As they run along the gully, they notice an empty bassinet racing along with them, bobbing and dipping in the crashing water. They slow down as they approach a tree trunk sticking out from the gully and blocking the path next to the retaining wall. The stump of what was left of the tree sank into the mud.

Kundu steps up on the short wall and walks over one limb and then under another. Lorraine follows behind him. Kundu jumps down to the path, splashing the overflowed water. Lorraine steps under the protruding limb, trodding on her recently sliced sole. She jerks then slips in the gully. She holds on to the edge with both hands. Her feet and legs are being pulled by the rush of the cold gully water. Kundu lunges and grabs both her hands. He plants both his knees into the wall and pulls her towards him. But everything is wet, and he can feel her slipping. An empty wooden drawer, floating swiftly crashes into the wall next to her. The gully is filled with pieces of everything, slamming ferociously on their way to the sea. Kundu tries to pull her up once more.

He bites his lip and pulls with his eyes closed. The water has risen and reaches Lorraine's chest.

Lorraine looks back at the water, then at the path leading from the hole in the fence. The shottas are running towards them along the path.

"Kundu. Kundu, them coming."

Kundu sees the last one coming through the hole and now running along the path.

"Let me go," cries Lorraine. Kundu shakes his head and holds her tight, grunting as he tries to lift her again.

"You see what them do to Peta-Gaye. I don't want that. Let me go. Please." Lorraine looks down, then back at Kundu.

"Then I coming with you," said Kundu desperately.

The shottas come to the fallen tree blocking the path and stop.

Another hand reaches from behind Kundu and grabs Lorraine by the armpit. Kundu looks up and sees Makka Beard above him. They pull Lorraine up onto the path. Makka Beard has a machine gun in his left hand. The shottas clear the fallen tree. Baby Face Shotta steps from behind.

"I think you was Rasta man. You have big gun like a war you declare," says Baby Face Shotta.

Kundu and Lorraine scurry behind Makka Beard.

"Where is Junjo? Him I want to talk to," says Makka Beard.

"Laborite them kill him off."

"So is what you want with the youth them?"

"A Ghost we want talk to."

Lorraine and Kundu look at each other.

"Well, hear this. 'Lowe them, leave them alone." Makka Beard declares.

"A one gun you have." Baby Face Shotta takes a step forward.

"Who want to die first? Just raise you hand. You see this place here, my turf this. You overstand. Because I a Rasta man don't mean say you can come chuck it, like you a Don. You see my locks? A no for pretty show. His Imperial Majesty say that the soldiers of Rastafari must have a dreadful appearance. Strike fear in the enemy before anything even start. Rasta no soft. Gwan about you business. Obeah woman can't save you."

Baby Face Shotta laughs, then spits in the running water, and turns his back to Makka Beard.

"See you soon."

The shottas walk behind Baby Face Shotta, back to the hole in the fence and jump through feet first.

"You have bad man gun?" asked Kundu.

"It empty. I find it yesterday. I go look for some water by Standpipe and I see it next to a man."

"Empty? What if them start to shoot?"

"All a we dead. But Jah is within I and I. But wait, where is Abednego? Is Shadrach, Meshach. Where is the other one?"

Kundu looks down. "Them shoot him. Get shot in him belly. Him dead."

"Who shoot him?"

"Laborite."

"Boy, them people here wicked man. Wicked bad."

The gully water splashes across them as they watch the last shotta jump through the hole.

A refrigerator and mattress float like cotton through the gully. The water surges to the top of the retaining wall. The rain had stopped completely, and everything was quiet except for the uneven banging of a Ford Granada pressed up against the walls.

Every piece of window, stove, roof, couch, and TV became alive in the Sandy Gully's up-and-down dance. Everything seems to rejoice on their way to some heavenly place. The old people that love the cricket would say 'God out for ducks.' Nothing good come out of a hurricane. It even worse when hurricane come to a place like Riverton City.

"What happen to Madda Tee? Makka Beard stands under his tarpaulin and calls Kundu and Lorraine to join him.

"The roof blow off. And she send us to the church." Kundu squeezes closer to the fence.

"I man used to fix the house for her, you know. When you mother go a Ocho Rios, everything just mash up."

Makka Beard adjusts his garbage bag raincoat. A big wave of brown gully water sprays across the tarpaulin and into the air. "Them send me go a general penitentiary. But me no do them things anymore. I sorry for the little youth still." Makka Beard shakes his head.

Chapter 52

Day After

The ground trembles for the first time in forty-eight hours. The Thames truck driven by the slender man in the straw hat and gold chains, rumbles through the main path. Its wheels crack and pop dog carcasses bloated with water. Fences that once stood proudly erect have disappeared into the night. The ones that remain are plastered in green 'JLP.' The fence across from Madda Tee's has 'Trinity de yah' splashed across the fence from one side to the next. The Thames belches smoke and growls as it tears through the scattered garbage newly infested with flies. Mosquitoes that favored the anonymity of sundown, bravely attach, suck then guzzle from uncovered arms, necks and buttocks. Everything was hungry.

Hordes of Riverton City squatters follow the Thames as it comes to a cross section. The driver makes a right turn up a slight hill passing the Church of Deliverance. He stops and back the truck up to the old pile that didn't crumble. He lifts the bed of the truck and dumps cement blocks, wet boxes, tree branches, steel rods, and shattered pieces of plywood chips. The disappointed murmurs are swift and grows louder as most observers turned and walked back to where they were standing. Some children climb the pile, looking for pipe, marbles and old toys. The driver with the straw hat stands next to his truck cabin, pulling the control lever that tilts and lifts the bed. His load falls off the raised flatbed, and some tumble down to the foot of the old pile. The driver lowers the truck's bed and jumps in the cabin.

A brown farmer's fruit bag rolls down to the base of the pile and pops open. The face of a primary schoolgirl pops out. Her eyes are closed and her mouth is covered with a black rope. Her teeth are missing and dried blood is crusted on her ear and jaw. The truck driver drives off, casually ploughing through the mud and deep holes of water. The truck followers shout and wave at the driver to stop, but he continues casually down the main path towards Standpipe.

The crowd behind the truck has grown, with more fingers pointing. A shirtless man, waving a machete, slaps the passenger door of the truck. There is a police lorry and a squad car partially blocking the path. Two of the six policemen carry Leon, wrapped in an army-green blanket and lay him into the back of the police lorry. Darlene climbs into the back of the lorry and sits next to Leon's head. Kundu and Lorraine are standing next to the partially ripped fence. Madda Tee and Ms. V are standing behind them.

A tall skinny man that plays his radio loudly when the West Indies play cricket, is talking to another police officer sitting in the car that is blocking the path of the Thames truck. The policeman gets out of his car and walks over to the driver's door, and the driver with the straw hat opens the door and steps down into the street. The police lorry with four policemen, Darlene and Leon, drives away slowly. Kundu steps out from the fence as Lorraine wipes tears from her eyes.

"The old demon yah a drop body up a di church. A him a kill the schoolgirl them," shouts the man with the machete. Big Joncrow birds fly slowly above everyone. Their giant wings are perfect for gliding and swooping for decaying food. They fly when they're hungry.

More onlookers get closer to the truck. The policeman raises his hand and motions to the crowd to stand back. The second police officer steps out of the passenger door and walks up to the Thames driver. He opens the door and hops into the truck.

"You have anything inside here?" asks the policeman, while rummaging through the seats and door pockets of the truck's cabin. He pulls a thin yellow panty from under the seat, then a polka dot red and white one. He looks under the seat again and pulls out more panties.

"See it dey! A him. Mek we kill him bomboclaat."

The policeman slaps the driver's straw hat from his head and grabs him by the waist and pant belt. He turns him around and push him against the truck, slamming his face against the door.

"Back off!" shouts the policeman standing behind the driver, waving off the crowd.

The policeman searching the cabin of the truck jumps out and walks around to his partner.

"A Blackheart Man this. Him fi dead! No mercy. Look how him mash up the likkle girl," says the Cricket man.

"A six girl?" says a woman's voice from behind the tall cricket man.

"No, a seven now. This one we just find make seven," yells the man with the machete.

Ms. V and Madda Tee step from behind the fence and pulls Kundu and Lorraine away from the crowd that had grown twice in size since the truck stopped. Two more men arrive with machetes and then another with a pick-ax. The murmurs and deep angry grumblings grow like a balloon, almost ready to explode into a frenzy that would ravage skin, flesh and bone. Shadows of more Joncrow birds glide above the swarm of people. Hands and voices are high. The crowd lunges and snaps like ferociously hungry hyenas, starved by drought and dust.

"Officer, officer. One girl a my sister. My sister," shouts a young man with the pick-ax. "Make we deal with it."

The growing crowd shifts closer and then jostles the police officer holding the driver. The policeman that found the panties under the seat of the truck, fires two shots in the air. Heads duck and shoulders cringe as wide eyes look around to see where the shots went.

The policeman handcuffs the truck driver and walks him to the back of the police car. The police man opens the rear passenger door. A rock hurls through the buzzing voices and crashes into the back of the driver's head. The policeman raises his gun again. The faces in the crowd twist, snarl, and crouch to the ground. Blood comes running down the back of the driver's head. His white mesh mariner is bright red with thick blood. The policeman pushes the driver into the back of the police car. The policemen, both hold their revolvers next to their ear while getting into the front seats of the car. The rear wheels of the police car slip through the mud and barely moves. The policeman puts the car in reverse and then drives forward quickly towards Standpipe.

Kundu, Lorraine, Madda Tee and Ms. V watch as the crowd follow the police car skidding and sliding in the mud.

Chapter 53

Ms. Gogo

The telephone bill was twelve hundred and fifty US dollars for the month of July alone. Ms. Gogo called Chengdu, China every day, sometimes six to nine times. The voice on the other end sounds like a young girl, maybe a teenager. The voice said her husband was not there, then silence, then a buzzing dial tone.

She used all the numbers in his Filofax planner to call every number listed. She called the numbers without names next to them. She would fall asleep at 3am, after she took her yellow pills. She would wash the pills down with a glass of Tia Maria and then black tea.

Ms. Gogo watched every morning as Millicent made breakfast with ackee and saltfish, sometimes okra and breadfruit with porridge for Butch. She walked him out to the car and he would rub her back right above her bottom. Millicent walked into the house with a smile. Ms. Gogo watched her or would listen to her footsteps to guess where she was in the house. No one came to see Ms. Gogo, and she didn't leave the house anymore. She rarely talked either.

Butch would ask her if she wanted to sit on the second-floor veranda. Sometimes she would turn her head halfway to look at him. He looked like his father, so she would smile and ask where he was all this time.

When her eyes cleared, Ms. Gogo would grab his hand and tell him she didn't like too many dark people around and on top of that, she doesn't want any black pickney a run around the place. Butch sat and listened. It was the only time she seemed alive and not too sad. She was better when she was angry.

Millicent brought her food and pills, and took her laundry.

Ms. Gogo sometimes asked for more pills. The red pills were for her headaches and eye pain, she said. Millicent brought them and gave them to her with her glass of Tia Maria.

You look like you mother, she said to Millicent. Ms. Gogo told Millicent that she was almost finished working off the money her mother owed. As Ms. Gogo stared through the window, she told Millicent that she can go back to Riverton City next week. Millicent fixed her pillow and pulled the shade to block the sun from Ms. Gogo's eyes.

Millicent stands at the door and tells her that her son Butch doesn't want a bastard child, so they got married at St. Richards Church. She holds up her left hand, where her ring finger sparkled with a thin gold band. The baby should be here in about seven months, Millicent told her. Ms. Gogo was going to be a grandmother. Ms. Gogo folded her body and cried, sniffling until mucus rolled from her small flat bridged nose.

Millicent walked out of Ms. Gogo's room with her shoulders pressed back. She walked to the kitchen and poured coco tea from a simmering pot left on the stove. She turns off the stove, sits down at the table in the kitchen. Millicent looks down at the tile where her mother died, and smiled.

Chapter 54

Ascension

The shottas circle aimlessly like mad ants in Peta-Gaye's abandoned yard. The grey cinder block and cement house is gone. Pieces of crumbled blocks are partly submerged in the mud. The shottas are dressed in white. They walk back and forth and around an old red pickup truck. Junjo's body is dressed in white pants, shirt and white pointed boots. His dark skin looks lime green against the white suit. There is a revolver in his left hand and bullets in the other.

Baby Face Shotta steps into the bed of the pickup truck. Horse Mouth Lucy sprinkles a mixture of dust and ashes across his face. A shotta standing away from the pickup and fires four shots in the air.

A crowd moves in from the main path, away from the next truck passing by. People begin to wander into the circle and look at Junjo laid out in the back of the pickup. Children hide behind the adults; they know there will be an explosion of gun fireworks coming soon. Madda Tee walks slowly towards the back of the pickup truck. Ms. V walks up behind her and puts her hand on Madda Tee's hunched shoulder. Madda Tee is still. She stares at Junjo's face. His mouth is twisted, as it would, before he'd let go of a smile. She walks to the side of the pickup, reaches over and rubs his forehead. Ms. V takes her hand and leads her away towards the growing crowd.

"Watch yah. I want everybody fi hold up a gun or a gun finger in di air. 'Ole it up!" shouts Baby Face Shotta. He continues after a drink from a Ray and Nephew Rum bottle.

"Junjo a my pardi. All a unu know dat. A him defend Riverton City from Laborite. The Laborite dem come kill him. So you know say a war dem a deal wid. A war dem declare. We neva go a Rema, we no go a Tivoli. We no bother nobody. Dem send di buoy Trinity come yah. And we duss him out. Him come wid big talk bout him a gargon and cyaa defend it. A we and Junjo do dat. In a England, them have Charles the second and Elizabeth the third, and name like that. From today, me a Junjo the Second. Don't call me no Baby Face. You understand me?"

He takes the silver handle gun from his waist and holds it above his head. He continues, "Gun salute to the original Junjo One."

He fires rapidly into the air. The shottas gathered around the pickup truck, and the others standing in the crowd, all fire their guns in a deafening symphony of explosions and smoke. Horse Mouth Lucy is staring towards Madda Tee and Ms. V. Kundu and Lorraine are standing behind them.

Two shottas spray the sky with loud rapid machine guns hoisted heavily on their shoulders. The smoke from the guns smells like burnt steel or a pot that had been left on the stove too long. Baby Face Shotta steps down from the bed of the pickup truck and points to a young shottas, who slides into the driver's seat of the pickup truck and slams the door. He then starts driving the pickup slowly through the crowd that gathered. Baby Face Shotta slows down as he sees Kundu standing behind Madda Tee, then Lorraine standing behind Ms. V.

"A me a run tings now. No worry you self. We not raising your rent," says Babyface Shotta, leaning in closer to Madda Tee's ear.

"If the dundus boy need a work, send him to me. Him can help you pay you tithes."

He continues to walk past her then looks at Kundu and Lorraine. He looks again at Kundu, then doubles over coughing violently, spitting saliva and blood. Horse Mouth Lucy pats his back. Kundu steps from behind Ms. V; his eyes are burgundy red. Lucy raises Baby Face Shotta by the shoulders and walks him away. She begins to cough heavily as she walks away with Baby Face Shotta, who looks back at Kundu as he wipes the spit and blood from his mouth. He smiles achingly, then walks away behind the procession and pickup truck carrying Junjo's body.

Chapter 55

No Place Like No Place

The neat, deliberately sectioned mountains of garbage were mostly flattened into each other. Hurricane Allan crushed twenty-foot-high, cone-shaped mountains into a ten-foot-high, almost flat, garbage swampland. Dead dogs with bloated bellies, now collecting big blue-winged flies, attract hungry Joncrow birds under a penetrating sun. The sky is clear now.

Radio Jamaica says that over two hundred people are unaccounted for. Much of the island is under water and with no electricity in many parishes. The Kingston Public Hospital didn't suffer any serious damage.

Epifanie was admitted one week before Allan. The doctors in Ocho Rios told her she was too sick for them to treat. She was wrapped in a blanket and placed in a medical minibus bound for downtown Kingston. After three hours, Epifanie arrived at KPH, twisting and shaking wildly. The nurses told her she had a fever of one hundred and three degrees. Two hours after her blood was drawn and sent to a lab, Epifanie was wheeled to the Hospice unit of KPH. Her bronze champagne skin had grown blisters around her lips and chin. She wasn't a tall woman, maybe five feet four. On her folder, affixed to a clipboard next to her bed, the nurse wrote 'eighty-six pounds'. The other patients in the Hospice ward lay steady. Except for the slow desperate breathing, nothing seems to be alive at all. The beds were cornered off by white and sometimes grey plastic shower curtains. There were six beds on each side of the long, narrow room. Next to the short single bed was a bedpan, an oxygen tank and a wooden crucifix above the bed. The floor pops and creaks when plastic-soled shoes walk across. The sheets, wall, curtains and floor smell of Dettol and old mop water. There were no windows to welcome sunlight. The doors were unmolested except for the hourly attending of the charge nurse. The doctors did not visit this ward.

Epifanie sinks into the bed on her side. Her lips are dry, cracked and parted enough to sip the Dettol air. Her fingers and face are thin. She can see her toes at the end of the bed sticking out from under the hospital cover sheet. The feet of the patient directly across from her bed are sticking out too. The right foot had only the pinky toe at the end. The rest was stitched shut. The left foot had all of its toes. The big toe leans far away from the second toe as if preparing to leave, and the heels are crusted with white dead skin. Nothing moved there, the bed, the plastic curtains on each side, no arms, no legs, everything was ready for the tomb.

Epifanie rolls over slowly, her face contorts and strains in pain. Her hair is random, like shrubs in a forest. Flakes from her scalp linger at the end, then fall perilously on her shoulders. The door to the ward opens, but the charge nurse, on her hourly survey, did not walk in as customary. Epifanie recognize the steady limp and the muffled grunt. Madda Tee surveys the bed with the missing toes and then stands next to Epifanie's bed.

"You turn Catholic now?" asks Madda Tee. She points to the crucifix on the wall.

Epifanie looks up above her head and sees the crucifix for the first time.

"Not mine. Is the hospital." says Epifanie. "How you know I was here?"

"V tell me. Somebody who clean here, see you name. Is a woman who use to live behind Standpipe."

"A you alone come?"

"You brother dead." Madda Tee exhales and sits halfway on Epifanie's bed.

"Moses." Epifanie's face quickly pales.

"Him and the shotta them in a war with the Laborite."

"When?"

"Hurricane night. Gun shot a fly every way. Him say him a defend PNP land."

Epifanie painfully shakes her head. "You sure? Cause mi no feel it. When something happen to him me feel it. Same way for him."

"The shotta them have gun salute funeral for him. You know they use to call him 'Junjo'?"

"I know."

"You brother turn Don. Collect money from everybody. Him say for protection and what's it not." Madda Tee brushes Epifanie's hair from her face. Tears roll down her nose, then across her chin.

"Mamma mi sorry. Mi wish mi could a tell you how mi sorry. Mi expect fi dead long time now."

Epifanie shakes her head from side to side. She grimaces as she tries to roll her body to lay flat on her back.

"Is not me. You no have to tell me sorry. You a big woman. A so life stay."

"Ten years I don't see you. I don't know Kundu. Nothing at all."

"Him outside."

"Outside now?"

"I bring him."

"I can't see him. How am I going to see him this way? Look pon mi." She pushes herself into the pillow and tries to sit up. She sinks back into the bed. "Him outside? Oh, God. What we going to say?"

"Tell him how it go. The truth," says Madda Tee.

"Him outside the door?"

Madda Tee rests the palm of her hand over Epifanie's shaking hand. She leans in closer. "What them say wrong with you?"

"Them say everything. Mi blood, liver, kidney, heart, sometime even mi head. I wi see colors and things that not really real. But it look real to me. A really you this mamma? And Kundu outside?"

"It real. I going to call him inside, alright?"

"No!" Epifanie's covers her face. "A shame, a shame, a shame, a shame."

Madda Tee rubs Epifanie's hand and consoles her. "I have to call him."

Epifanie is resigned. "Ok. You right. Call him."

Madda Tee dismounts slowly from the bed and clears the rigid plastic curtains. Epifanie listens while Madda Tee's feet drag and clop towards the door. The door hinges creak and then fall silent. Epifanie brushes her hair back and wipes her face with her fever-warm hands.

Madda Tee walks back into the ward with Kundu next to her. He is wearing government school-issued khaki pants, blue shirt, and dull brown shoes. The shoes are two sizes bigger than his feet. Madda Tee and Kundu stand at the foot of Epifanie's bed.

Epifanie stares at him then buries her head in her hands and weeps. Madda Tee turns and walks away and through the door. Epifanie wipes her face with her hands. Kundu looks down at his shoes and clasp his hands behind his back, as if standing in his school assembly.

"You start school already?" asked Epifanie.

"No. Next week."

"You look like you going to school."

"This the clean clothes I have."

"You look neat and handsome."

Kundu looks down at his shoes. "Thank you."

"You tall, too. You can sit here if you want." Epifanie points to the place where Madda Tee sat. Kundu walks to the side of the bed, but stands assembly style.

"You no remember me don't?" asked Epifanie.

"Maybe, I think so. A little bit."

"That's alright. You was one when I leave. You eleven now."

Kundu hesitates. "How come you leave? Is because people laugh when them see mi?"

"No, no. That no have nothing to do with it." Epifanie struggles to sit up. "You a my son. Mi neva care what nobody want to say. You a my son." Kundu finally sits softly beside her.

The woman with the four missing toes across from Epifanie, coughs deeply then rolls on to her stomach. Her remaining six toes point towards the sticky floor. Kundu and Epifanie stay still as the woman repositions and then settles into the indent she created.

"Madda Tee say you coming back fi me," Kundu says quietly. "But you never come."

"Mi did plan fi make some money, but tings neva work the way mi think. All now mi no have even a fardin to mi name, not even a penny. Mi couldn't even look pon you."

"Them call me duppy and ghost," he whispered, "And mi no have no mother or father."

"You have a mother. You have a father."

Kundu looks up at Epifanie. His white eyebrows narrow towards the center of his face.

"Who that?"

"Moses."

"Who is Moses?"

"Junjo."

"Junjo name is Moses?"

"Yes. Madda Tee son. My twin brother."

Epifanie takes a deep breath, but coughs as she exhales. Kundu looks back at the door that Madda Tee exited. Epifanie coughs again. Kundu looks back into her sunken eyes.

"Him dead. Them say Trinity shot him."

Epifanie wheezed out. "I know."

"How come him no say so?"

"Maybe him no want nobody do anything to you cause a him. If him a don, and somebody no like him, maybe them come after you, if them know say you a him son. Understand?"

Kundu nods his head. "Me and my friend them see him all the time. Him a shotta."

Epifanie covers her mouth and tears roll down her face once again. "You have friends? Who you friends?"

"I use to have two, but one get shot. Leon. Leon get shot in him belly."

"Leon? Darlene son? You and him born about the same time. I know Darlene long time. Oh God, poor Darlene. Leon dead. And you and him was friends." Epifanie reaches out and grasps his hand.

She holds it up, inspecting the scratches and bruises along his arm and hand. His fingernails are discolored with dirt. His eyes are more purple than hazel now, and she could make out the quizzical arch in his platinum blond eyebrows. The armpit of his shirt is darkened with sweat.

"I have another friend. She waiting outside. Them say she can't come in because she not your daughter. She name Lorraine."

"Lorraine?"

"She pass her Common Entrance exam. She going to skip six grade and go to high school. She going to Immaculate Girls School. She going to live there. I have to take the exam next year. If I pass I want to go to Calabar. Me and Leon was going to go there, but him can't go now. So a just me."

"What you going to be when you turn into a man?"

Kundu looks down at his shoes again.

"Is alright if you don't know. I did want to be a movie star," says Epifanie. Kundu smiles. Epifanie sees his chalk-white teeth for the first time. "Yes, I wanted to live in Hollywood. That's where they make the movies. You like movies?"

"Yes. I watch kung fu movies. Leon and me used to go to State Theater. Him have a cousin that use to let us in. We never have to pay anything. Leon was going to be a kung fu master. He was training in the yard."

"What do you want to be?" asked Epifanie again.

"I want to fly plane. I want to go up and fly into the sky. Far, far up." Kundu's face lights up. "When I walk to market, I see the plane them land and take off. Is like them a bird. Them can go anywhere."

"Larks, my son want to turn in a pilot."

"Them say mi eye bad. The school eye doctor say dundus no have perfect eye. When the sun too bright, mi can't see. So mi can't turn pilot. Lorraine say when she turn doctor, she will fix mi eyes for me."

"Nothing no wrong with you. You don't have to listen to them people. If you want to turn pilot, you can turn pilot. Learn you lesson a school. Mi no want you end up like you father, or me. Him dead and me deh yah in a dead ward. No mi son, you better than we."

The ward door swings open, and the charge nurse walks into the room. She's dressed in a white uniform, white stockings, crisp white shoes, and white meshed bonnet.

"Oh!" She gasps as Kundu looks out at her from behind the curtain. "Oh, Lawd have his mercy. You frighten me. What you doing in here?"

"This is my mother," says Kundu.

"It's my son," says Epifanie, looking at him.

"Ok. Well, you have to come back another day. We have ward check right now," replies the nurse.

"Alright." says Epifanie. The nurse opens the door and stands under the frame.

"Bye-bye." Kundu turns to walk to the door, then turns back quickly to Epifanie. He takes her thin hand and kisses it on the back. Epifanie strains her face but couldn't find the strength to move. She falls back deeper into the bed.

"Everything alright. Tell Madda Tee thanks. She will know." As Kundu walks out of the room, Epifanie opens her mouth wide. She screams with no sound, her hands gripping the mattress and sheets beneath her. The charge nurse closes the door behind Kundu as he walks out.

Chapter 56

Five Hundred Miles

An armada of yellow bulldozers rumble through the main path, pushing and ploughing through the new landscape of infinite garbage. Before the truck could return, the old piles must be rebuilt and labeled for fresh dumping. The shacks along the way that were empty and too close to the path, were crushed and removed too.

Without a yard and someone to call him, Jomo wandered through the narrow lanes that stood up against the power of Hurricane Allan. He and the small naked children search for apples and squashed brown bananas.

Madda Tee's fence was rebuilt, but was six feet closer to her one-room shack. Makka Beard re-attached her zinc roof after he added new zinc to Ms. V's roof. He and Ms. V found pieces of zinc stranded on the causeway. Makka Beard knew about carpentry from his father. His father used to build furniture for people who wanted something unique. For a small amount, Makka Beard would help the squatters rebuild and start over. He helped Madda Tee, even though she briefly blamed him for Epifanie's pregnancy.

It's Monday morning at eight-thirty and the sun is already hard at work. Kundu and Lorraine are walking to the X77 bus stop along the highway. Lorraine has the crocus bag that Ms. V gave her for the clothes she had. She was wearing a long grey frock that stopped at the ankles. Madda Tee said the Catholics don't like to see too much skin pon a young lady. Kundu is carrying an old backpack they found in the flat pile. It was dry and only had one broken zipper. She placed the books and shoes she had in the backpack.

"You know where it is?" asks Kundu.

"Not really. But Ms. V say to ask the bus driver. Them know where everything is."

"You have you own bathroom inside the place?"

"Millicent say them have toilets that flush," said Lorraine excitedly.

"You can come out when you want?"

"No. The nuns only let you out holiday time. I have to stay there."

Kundu nods. "Yeah, that better than coming back down here."

The car path from the main road is empty. The women in shorts and bikini tops that walk back and forth, greeting strangers in cars, are gone. Cars, minibuses, bikes and trucks bore through the intersection. Lorraine and Kundu scamper across the street and stand next to the crowd waiting to get on the X77.

"You taking the Common Entrance next year. You ready?" asks Lorraine.

"I'm going to study. Study hard. My mother say that."

"Yes, pass and go to big school. You want to go a Calabar. You have to study."

Kundu sounds unsure. "But mi no bright like you."

"You ever see me make kite?" Lorraine puts her hand on his shoulder. "Me couldn't make nothing like what you make."

"I'm going to study hard. Maybe I can come check you at Immaculate."

"Only girls can come into the school."

Kundu looks down at his shoes. The crowd gathered by the bus stop begin to cluster tighter along the edge of the sidewalk.

"The bus is coming," says Kundu.

"Ok. You remember what I asked you to promise me?"

"Asked me?"

"Yes, you. Who else is here?" She smiles, then gets serious in her eyebrows.

"What you say?"

"Don't turn shotta."

"Me not turning shottas."

"Promise me." Lorraine looked directly into Kundu's eyes.

Kundu paused; she was serious. "I promise I'm not turning shotta."

"Cross you heart?"

"Cross my heart."

"Hope to die."

"Hope to die."

The bus stops in front of the impatient crowd. They file in one by one. Kundu puts the backpack on Lorraine's shoulders, and she steps up onto the bus. She walks all the way to the back of the bus with her bags and sits next to the open window. An open window usually warns of a broken air conditioning system.

Lorraine sits with her bag on her lap and the backpack still on her back. She looks away to the other side of the bus and wipes her face. Kundu inspects his shoes, then looks up at her, squinting with glossy purple eyes. The passengers sitting on that side of the bus are looking intently at Kundu too.

The doors of the bus close and it slowly rolls away from the curb.

Kundu walks along with the bus as the driver waits as a man on a cart pulled by a donkey crosses the street. As the bus speeds up Kundu shouts, but Lorraine can't hear him. He runs faster to catch up to the window.

"Hill and gully rider," shouts Kundu.

Lorraine smiles a big grin and leans towards the window. "Hill and gully."

"Hill and gully rider." The bus is moving faster.

"Hill and gully," calls out Lorraine.

Kundu is running as hard as he can. "Hill and gully rider."

The driver changes gears, and the bus pulls away.

"Hill and gully," grins Lorraine.

Kundu stands by the side of the road, waving at Lorraine. As the bus speeds away into distant traffic, Kundu turns and walks slowly back towards the bus stop. He couldn't explain what he was feeling. His eyes burned with salt of his tears, and his stomach felt like he ate something rotten.

He promised Makka Beard to help him work on the shacks and rooms ripped up by Hurricane Allan. Kundu walked back to Riverton City, thinking of his friends and trying to hide the tears that would not stop.

Chapter 57

Letter To Gurty

New fences are being constructed everywhere the eye can see. Some yards are occupied by the same squatters before Allan, and others by new squatters making a claim by re-building first.

A steady parade of dump trucks roar their way through the new dump route. The load scouts call out the content of the truck, barking out if it's food or lumber, construction parts or oil containers. Dogs, children, and professional scavengers ambush the truck as it speeds through the alleys, now widened by the giant bulldozer sent by Kingston Public Works and the Office of Sanitation.

Horse Mouth Lucy stands next to a new fence, watching Kundu as he retrieves a market bag filled with semi-old guineps. Since Allan, Horse Mouth Lucy was always somewhere near Kundu. She had a bag of dried dog bones slung around her neck. She would look, but pretend she wasn't looking. She did not look Kundu in the eye anymore. Her coughing grew deeper and with blood sometimes.

Madda Tee told Kundu the time had come for her to go to Florida. Her sister Gurty paid for a stowaway spot on the Scirocco. It is the same ship that carry Gurty to America, she told him. Ms. V is going to take over Madda Tee's little house when she leaves. That way, Kundu will have somebody looking after him and have a place to sleep.

"Listen me," says Madda Tee. She gives him a crocus bag she packed with clothes the day before. "I have to go on the ship early, so is tonight, after eight tonight."

Kundu wraps loose strings around the stem of the guineps, separating them in dozens. He doesn't say anything. Kundu sits on his heels atop a single box frame he found after Allan. It was still slightly wet.

Madda Tee continues, "Help me carry the bag them. Ms. V coming to send me off."

"Don't worry, Madda Tee. I'm going to study hard and go to Calabar."

"You not my born son, but you a still my son. I know people make you feel a way, but a because them no know you. Plus some of them no have no sense. From the minute you born, that mean that God bless you. You know how much people no born? If God put you pon this earth that mean say you bless. And who God bless, nobody can curse. Remember that."

They walk out into the yard. Kundu has the bag with clothes over his shoulder. Makka Beard climbs down from Ms. V's roof and walks behind them through the gate.

Madda Tee, Kundu, Makka Beard and Ms. V walk slowly along the causeway as the sun sets. Madda Tee is wearing her favorite white blouse with the ruffled neck, and blue jeans with brown plastic sandals. Ms. V is wearing her cleaner's uniform from KPH. Her red toe-slippers 'clip clop' with every step she takes. Madda Tee told Kundu to look decent when him sending somebody off to foreign. So he wears his khaki pants and school shirt like he did for the hospital. Makka Beard is wearing his highwater jeans, with construction boots and white mesh undershirt. He has a hammer in his waist.

Lagging behind them is a constellation of Joncrow birds, swooping and hovering above the freshly carved dump pile, rich with decay. Smoke billowed from a dump that caught on fire.

Madda Tee walks slower than before, each step summoning a grimace across her face.

After thirty minutes, they stop at the bus shed for the X77, but going in the opposite direction of the bus Lorraine took to Immaculate. The bus is half full. Madda Tee and Ms. V sit next to each other. Kundu sits next to Makka Beard.

The driver is a burly woman, with big thick arms that bulge out of her short sleeve uniform. There is no conductor on the bus. Passengers sit, looking out the windows as the bus levitates and bounces towards the orange sunset. Ms. V rings the bell, alerting the driver to stop at the dock. Madda Tee stands up and Kundu helps her to steady herself down the steps. Makka Beard and Ms. V walk slowly behind Madda Tee and Kundu.

The dock is empty, but for the black and white ship with many containers stacked atop each other. The bus pulls away slowly and then speeds off. Kundu has both bags. They walk to the ladder leading to the deck. Two men are standing behind a knotted rope. Madda Tee takes out her letter from her purse.

"Gurty send this," she says to the taller of the two olive-skinned men. She hands him the paper.

The two men are both dressed in white short sleeved shirts, black tie, black pants and black shoes.

"A you the captain?" asks Madda Tee.

"Yes" says the taller man. He continues, "this is for one person."

"Yes, for one person. Him." Madda Tee points to Kundu.

Ms. V turns her back to them. Makka Beard stands still, but inspects the hull of the ship.

"Me?" Kundu is shocked.

"You have to go. You can't stay here," said Madda Tee. "Shotta a look for you. The obeah woman a follow everywhere you go. You can go live with Gurty. She is you grand aunt. I talk to you mother already; she can't do nothing for you. You see her, she not managing."

Kundu stares at his grandmother. "What about you? You want to go America. Remember?"

The older woman shakes her head. "What me going to do there? Me can hardly walk. Mi too old. If I stay down here, at least mi know people, mi can manage. You can go, get your papers and come back when you want."

Kundu starts to cry and puts his arms around Madda Tee. "No, Madda Tee. I will clean up the yard better. Madda Tee, I'm going to study hard so I can go to Calabar. A promise." She puts his head on her shoulder. "Madda Tee, Madda Tee."

Madda Tee rubs his head and rocks him the way she rocked him as a child. "You have to be brave, Kundu." Madda Tee takes his head and looks in his eyes. His white eyebrows are furrowed, thick tears roll from his purple eyes.

She pulls his bag over his shoulders. "You have blessing. America don't care about dundus. A whole lotta white people have white eyebrow and red hair. Some them have blue eye, and sometime grey or hazel."

Ms. V turns around. Her eyes are red and watery. "Gwaan, Kundu," she urges him. "The clothes in the bag is yours."

Makka Beard is still inspecting the hull.

Madda Tee lets him go and steps back. "Ms. Gurty going to meet you at the dock." says his grandmother. She hugs him again. "Mi love you till mi dead. You understand?"

Kundu nods his head as tears continue to roll down his cheeks. He steps onto the ladder leading to the deck. The men walk behind him as he walks up. Madda Tee watches as he gets to the top. Ms. V waves again.

"Come, Madda Tee," Makka Beard cautions. "We have to catch the last bus back to Three Mile. Come."

Kundu stands on the forward stern and watches as Madda Tee, Makka Beard and Ms. V walk towards the bus stop. They cross the empty causeway and stand next to the sign for the easterly X77. Kundu looks out and across the Kingston harbor and then back at Madda Tee, Ms. V, and Makka Beard. Kundu's face is tight from the dried tears and sweat. The X77 appears suddenly, and blocks Kundu's view. The bus rocks from side to side then moves slowly away from the curb. Kundu watches the white top of the bus roll away, and then turn out of sight.

Madda Tee and Ms. V sit side by side. Makka Beard sticks his head out of the window and raises his fist in the air. Madda Tee, falls to her knees on the bus floor, holding her stomach and crying. Ms. V crouches next to her and puts her arm around her shoulders, comforting her oldest friend. Kundu looks across the Kingston harbor; he could also see the airstrip of Tinson Penn airport.

A yellow and white Cessna is taking off. Kundu locks his eyes on the plane as it rises into the sky and disappears into the low hanging white clouds. In an instant, he remembers walking past the airstrip with Leon and Lorraine.

"Hill and gully rider, hill and gully
Hill and gully rider, hill and gully
Hill and gully rider, hill and gully."

Kundu stood still, assembly style, as the ship slowly sailed away from the dock. The breeze blew over and through his body.

He felt as if he held out his arms, he could fly.

The End

About the Author

Author Courtney Ffrench is the Artistic Director of the Jamaica Center for Arts and Learning in Southeast Queens, New York. Born in Kingston, Jamaica, Courtney moved to the United States in his teens, leaving his family behind. In his professional experience, Courtney has been an adoption specialist for children in foster care, and a middle school educator.

His personal philosophy embraces art as a vital component in the growth of the human experience. The quest to explore art manifested out of his discovery of underground after-hours dance clubs: dance became the essential vehicle of artistic expression. He then went on to tour with international pop star Irene Cara, and Lisa Lisa of Cult Jam. Through dance, Courtney went on to travel throughout Europe, Asia and the USA for several years as a dancer, producer, and choreographer.

Mr. Ffrench is also the founder and director of the Vissi Dance Theater. Their signature style combined the discipline of modern dance with the freedom of underground social dance. Courtney is featured in the dance documentary *Check Your Body At The Door*, by dance historian Sally Somers. Mr. Ffrench has always had a propensity for drama, theater and the musicality of words. Courtney has written two plays, *Just Us* and *The Rape of Henry Mudd*. He is also the author of a novel, *Tides and Tears*.

Kundu: The Prince of Riverton City is Mr. Ffrench's second novel.